Treveth

A Cornish

Volume 1

William Davy Watson

Alpha Editions

This edition published in 2024

ISBN : 9789362096029

Design and Setting By
Alpha Editions
www.alphaedis.com
Email - info@alphaedis.com

Contents

VOLUME 1

CHAPTER I.

"What, am I poor of late?
'Tis certain, greatness, once fallen out with fortune,
Must fall out with men too. What the declined is,
He shall as soon read in the eyes of others,
As feel in his own fall: for men, like butterflies,
Show not their mealy wings but to the summer;
And not a man, for being simply man,
Hath any honour; but honour for those honours
That are without him, as place, riches, favour,
Prizes of accident as oft as merit."

SHAKSPEARE.

Late in September, some thirty years ago, Henry Trevethlan lay dying in the state-bedchamber of Trevethlan Castle; in Cornwall. It was a large and lofty apartment, indifferently lighted by Gothic casements overlooking the sea, and wearing a gloomy and desolate aspect. Old hangings of tapestry, much faded and worn, covered the walls; the furniture was scanty and inconvenient; the floor was bare, and the dark oak had lost its polish; the very logs in the spacious chimney seemed damped by the cheerlessness of the room, and threw a dull red glare over the prodigious bed, where death was silently counting the few sands yet remaining in the upper half of his hour-glass.

As soon as he found himself seriously ill, Mr. Trevethlan had solemnly charged his medical attendant to warn him of the first approach of danger; and immediately that the announcement was made, he caused himself to be removed from the smaller but more commodious apartment which he usually occupied, to the dreary greatness of the state-chamber, taking no heed of the remonstrance that the change would probably hasten his dissolution.

"Pshaw!" said he. "What matter a few days? The Trevethlans always die in the state-rooms."

Accordingly their present representative was duly observing the custom. Four days had elapsed since his removal, and he had sunk so rapidly, that it was now doubtful whether as many more hours remained to him; but his mental faculties were still clear and unclouded. His son and daughter watched mournfully by his bedside.

"Helen," he said, "Helen Trevethlan, I wish to speak with your brother. Leave us for a while."

The girl rose silently, and glided out of the room. As soon as she had closed the door, the dying man turned feebly upon his pillows, fixed his still bright eyes upon his son, and spoke in low but distinct accents:

"Randolph, I leave you a beggar and a Trevethlan! May my curse cling to you, if ever you suffer poverty to tamper with pride. Employment will be open to you: may your appointment be your death-warrant. Ay, methinks it may raise my ghost, if Randolph Trevethlan accept a favour from Philip Pendarrel. Live, sir, here, as I have lived. Marry, sir, as I married. Rear an heir to the castle, as I have reared you. Bequeath him the same legacy, which I bequeath you. But there is my fear. How much of your mother's blood runs in your veins? What base leanings may you not have inherited from her? Feel you not a love for your peasant relatives? Gratifying my revenge by engrafting a wild bud on a noble stem, I forgot that the fruit might degenerate. Speak, sir, is it so? Do the honours of Trevethlan descend upon a dastard? Say it, that a father's curse may embitter the remainder of your days."

"Oh, my father," said the young man, in deep and earnest tones, "never shall our name be degraded while it belongs to me. But may I not strive to restore it to splendour? Must Trevethlan ever be desolate? Shall the successors of our race wander in these halls, only to mourn over their decay? And is the livery of office the sole passport to the means of renovation? Have I not hands, and a head, and heart?"

"What would you, sir?" exclaimed the father. "Hands! would you dig? There speaks your peasant mother. Head! learning! profession! What portrait has its face turned to the wall in yonder gallery? Mr. Justice Trevethlan, attaint of corruption. Heart! arms! Ay, but not in peace. No Trevethlan wears a sword to adorn a levee. And now, sir, the source of your commission would make it a disgrace."

"My father," Randolph again said, "to no patron will I be indebted for advancement. On myself alone I rely. May I not exert the powers I derive from nature? I thought not of the army: a uniform has no temptations for me. But, gazing on the back of that picture, might I not hope to wipe out the stain incurred in a corrupt age, by rising to be an example in purer times?"

"Shall a Trevethlan descend among the paltry Chiquanous?" said the dying man, with great bitterness. "Shall that name be mingled with the low trickery of the modern forum; exposed to the risk of failure, and to the mockery of upstart talent? Shall Esther Pendarrel smile at the rude eloquence of her rejected suitor's heir, and exult over the unretrieved ruin of his house? No, sir. Think it not. Starve, sir, here in Trevethlan Castle."

"But my father," the young man urged, "if means could be found whereby all such risk should be avoided; if success might restore our house, while failure could not degrade it; might I not venture on a career so guarded?"

"How, sir, is such a course practicable?"

"By permitting me, my father, for a time to wear a mask," answered Randolph. "The name of Trevethlan may be supposed to be wandering abroad, while the estates are recovering themselves at home; and the real bearer of the name, assuming one less known, may live obscurely in London, struggling honourably for an independence. If he fail, the pilgrim returns: if he succeeds, he brings new honour to Trevethlan Castle."

Mr. Trevethlan made no answer to this proposition for a considerable time; and his son might see by the varying expression of his sharpened features, the struggle which agitated his mind. At length he spoke, in tones milder and more parental than he had used previously.

"Randolph, I consent. I have watched you well, and, in spite of the taunts which break from my soured heart, I believe you are worthy of your name."

"Father," said the son, "my life must show my gratitude: it shall be passed, as if you still beheld it."

Again there was a long silence in the gloomy chamber. Then the dying man spoke anew, in accents still tenderer than his last.

"Randolph, I mentioned Esther Pendarrel. You know her not by sight. She was once, or I fancied she was, very dear to me. She coquetted with me, discarded me, and wedded my kinsman. I never forgave her; and, except on one provision, I now forbid all future intercourse with her or hers. But I have sometimes thought I was not so indifferent to her, as she, in her contempt, pretended. If it were so, she has avenged me on herself, and has my pardon. You know my dying will. As I have consented to the temporary obscuration of our race, so do you promise, with the qualification I mentioned, to have no friendly relations with the family of Philip Pendarrel."

Rashly and wrongfully the son gave the pledge wrongfully and deliberately required by the father, and soon afterwards summoned his sister back to her place beside the bed of death. The following morning the blinds were not raised in the windows of the castle, and the ragged flag which waved over the loftiest watch-tower, floated from the middle of its staff. The last sand of the hour-glass had run, and Henry Trevethlan was numbered with his fathers.

Trevethlan Castle was an extensive pile of Tudor architecture, situate on a bold headland projecting into the sea between the Lizard and Marazion. The state apartments stretched along the cliff, and commanded a fine view of Mount's Bay and the surrounding uplands; while the other buildings of the castle, strengthened at intervals by lofty towers, enclosed an irregular court-yard. The remains of walls and ruined turrets, sweeping inland, marked the circuit of what had once been the base-court—a spacious area, where Owen Trevethlan mustered his vassals to pursue Perkin Warbeck's rebels, obtaining for his services on that occasion the title of baron. This honour had, however, been allowed to lapse; and, although it was stated to be easily recoverable, no subsequent head of the family had chosen to moot the question. Perhaps they thought their name sufficiently distinguished without any addition: perhaps the fact that, being a crotchetty race, they were almost always in opposition to the Crown, made them loth to seek even the shadow of a favour.

But the days of feudal violence and civil dudgeon were long gone by; and instead of the clang of arms and the tramp of soldiers, the base-court of Trevethlan Castle now echoed no sound more military than the occasional crack of a fowling-piece; and its silence was more generally broken by the mower sharpening his scythe, or the gardener trailing a roller. Sooth to say, even these peaceful noises had been very rare for a long time previous to the opening of this tale: the garden which occupied the old place of arms had fallen into neglect; the ivy, which might have been ornamental to the ruined walls and outworks, stifled the trees and shrubs in its oppressive embrace; the flowers struggled hard for life amidst a host of weeds; the grass of the lawn, unmown since the summer, when it was cut for hay, was rusty and patchy; the gravel walks were green and mouldy. One little plot of ground, however, was an oasis in the general desert: it occupied an angle of the castle, having a southern aspect, and was screened from the sea-breezes by the wall along the cliff: here trim flower-beds were cut in a small expanse of turf, and displayed, even at this advanced season, not a few gems of horticulture.

And two or three windows, looking from the first floor on this still blooming garden, presented no less striking a contrast to the rest of the castle, than the garden itself afforded to the remainder of the great court. Their florid decorations were sharp and fresh; their glass was bright and clear; and white curtains within might temper the radiance of the mid-day sun. But, everywhere else, the progress of decay was manifest: the Gothic tracery was crumbling away; panes were frequently wanting in the casements; and when they were perfect, the winter spray and summer dust had rendered them nearly opaque. Weeds grew between the stones and on the ledges of the walls; and long creeping-plants hung from the battlements, and waved mournfully in the wind. Desolation reigned paramount over Trevethlan Castle.

Nor did the interior of the building belie its external aspect. The state bed-chamber was a sample of all the rest. In many of the rooms the dust had been undisturbed for nearly thirty years. But two were exceptions to the general neglect: one, the gallery to which Mr. Trevethlan referred, where hung the portraits of the family, generation after generation, from the days of Holbein to those of Reynolds. This was the favourite walk of Mrs. Griffith, the wife of the steward, whose office had been hereditary in his family almost from the earliest of those portraits. Mrs. Griffith used to spend much of her spare time in the gallery, walking to and fro with a long flapper of feathers in her hand, gently and reverentially brushing the dust from the pictures, and never passing that which was turned to the wall without a deep sigh.

The last Mrs. Trevethlan—a new Griselda—had been treated with civil neglect by her husband, and died under the weight of her position, after bearing him the son and daughter already introduced. She was the child of a small tenant upon the estate; and Mr. Trevethlan, having attained the only object of his marriage, checked some presumption of her family with marked disdain. The maternal care and early education of his children devolved upon Mrs. Griffith, and the portrait-gallery was their usual school-room. Here they learned the history of their family as the history of England: not a bad *memoria technica*, but one attended with some risk. However, it may easily be guessed that they had no hard task-mistress, and that battledore-and-shuttlecock often interrupted the story of Queen Elizabeth's maid-of-honour, or of the colonel who fell in endeavouring to rally Fairfax's horse at Marston Moor.

And whatever family pride might be acquired in this gallery was chastened in the other apartment exempted from the general desolation. This was the library, the especial domain of Polydore Riches, the chaplain of the castle. Riches held a fellowship at Cambridge, but had incurred, no matter how, the dislike of his superiors; being somewhat timid and retiring, he thereupon gave up residence, and accepted Mr. Trevethlan's offer of his chaplaincy and the curacy of the hamlet. And when that gentleman's affairs became inextricably involved, the worthy clergyman declined a release from his duties, and continued to reside at Trevethlan, maintaining himself on the proceeds of his fellowship. The people at the village said he might sometimes be seen in the dusk of evening, leaning on the tombstone in their churchyard which marked the resting-place of Rose Griffith, a relation of the steward. It was also said that he had positively refused to perform the marriage ceremony between his patron and Margaret Basset; and it was true. For once, Mr. Trevethlan respected a pride that was equal to his own, and contented himself with a sarcasm on the eccentricity of poverty.

Polydore had now resided nearly thirty years at the castle, and was more than fifty in age. But time sat light upon him, and he looked much younger. From Mrs. Griffith he received as pupils his patron's children, and the library took the place of the picture gallery. Polydore was enthusiastic, and children love enthusiasm: there was a tinge of sadness in his demeanour, and childish pity is more akin to affection than that of older persons. It was not wonderful that Randolph and Helen were frequently glad to escape from the presence of the cold and stern man whom they called father, to the teaching of the tender and gentle being who ruled in the library. Nor was it more strange that with such an instructor they made rapid proficiency in whatever pursuit he directed.

"Lonely," he exclaimed one day, when Randolph, then sixteen, inquired if he did not feel so in the solitude of the castle, "lonely with a library like this! Lonely in the society of those around me! Of Park, first beholding the Niger! Of Columbus, seeing the light from the poop of his ship! Of Watt, contemplating one of our Cornish engines! Of Newton, observing the fall of the apple! Of Luther, taking his stand at the Diet of Worms! Of Shakspeare, giving

'to airy nothing
A local habitation and a name!'

Of Bacon, writing 'Thus thought Francis of Verulam!' Lonely amidst the triumphs of enterprise, art and science; of history, poetry and philosophy! Lonely, where whatever science has discovered, and art applied, and enterprise accomplished; what history has recorded, and poetry exalted, and philosophy ordered, is visibly presented! Where power, skill, and understanding, memory, fancy, and wisdom have written their greatest names, their mightiest deeds, their noblest thoughts! No, Randolph Trevethlan, there is no loneliness in such society as this."

It was his own feeling, perhaps, that Randolph expressed in the inquiry which extracted this speech from the chaplain. For to the buoyancy of youth, the castle might well seem a dreary abode. When a man gives up the world, the world generally returns the compliment; and in this instance Mr. Trevethlan's violation of the bienséances in his marriage widened the breach. No friend or relation visited him during the last years of his life. And, indeed, their entertainment would have been a serious burden on the finances of their host. It is probable that the steward was a much richer man than his master; it is not impossible that all the expenses of Trevethlan did not fall upon its lord.

Yet the establishment had gradually declined to the lowest point. An old porter, named Jeffrey, who occupied the entrance lodge to the inner court, and cultivated a small kitchen garden, was the only male domestic: his wife, and two or three maid-servants performed all the other offices of the castle. People often wondered that Mr. Griffith did not leave such a falling house. But Mr. Griffith was not a rat. He had lived there more than half a century, and was prepared to continue as long again.

Nor let it be supposed that this devotion was entirely due to the place. Proud and reserved as had been its recent master, he was far from being wholly unamiable; even his children, to whom he behaved with uniform harshness, regarded him with as much affection as awe; and his dependents, whom he treated with almost as constant kindness, served him with real attachment. Well did Griffith recollect the day, although it was five and thirty years past, and he was scarcely twenty at the time, when Mr. Trevethlan galloped into the court-yard with his horse in a foam, on his return from Pendarrel, ordered his carriage, paced impatiently up and down the great hall while it was being prepared, and departed to London without uttering another word. Well, too, did the steward remember his father's grief, as missive after missive came to Trevethlan in the few following years, of which the constant burden was "money, money." Mortgage Tresylty, sell Penrevil, fell Withewood; so it went on, until the extensive domain, once appended to the castle, was reduced to its immediate precincts. Then Mr. Trevethlan came home, and lived during the remainder of his days in the secluded manner, which has already been sufficiently described.

CHAPTER II.

"Strange is it, that our bloods,
Of colour, weight, and heat, poured all together,
Would quite confound distinction, yet stand off
In differences so mighty."

SHAKSPEARE

Randolph Trevethlan was just of age when his father died; his sister, two years younger. Their singular education had impressed peculiarities upon each of them; but, trained so entirely together, their habits and dispositions had grown into a conformity almost perfect. Their pursuits, their wishes, their attachments were always the same. Their father never allowed them to set foot on any ground which had been alienated from the castle; and as such surrounded it at a short distance, their inland walks were restricted within a very narrow cordon. But the beach, no man's land, was open to their rambles: a winding stair led from the castle to a portal cut in the face of the rock on which it stood, and a flight of steps descended from this doorway to the shingles, washed by the waves which rolled eternally from the farthest Atlantic. Not far to the south, the rock formed a narrow promontory of inconsiderable height, but running out some distance into the sea. The rough granite afforded good footing, and with a little exertion, it was not difficult to reach the extremity, where there was a small cave. Randolph smoothed the ruggedness of the way, and this recess, which they called Merlin's Cave, became the favourite resort of himself and Helen. From it, they looked straightforward past Mousehole and the Logan Rock to the meeting of sea and sky, while a turn to the right, showed them St. Michael's Mount and the beautiful woods over Penzance. Here, in the warm season, they often sat for many hours together, reading the legends of Cornubia, and of Armorica across the waters. Here, in the winter, when the wind blew heavily from the west, they came to admire the huge swell of the ocean thundering idly on the granite beneath their feet. It might be thought that such a life would produce a dreamy and feeble turn of mind, ill-calculated to withstand the buffets of the world. And it will be found, in fact, that this result did in some degree follow. But the lessons and conversation of Polydore Riches, and the cold cynicism of Mr. Trevethlan, furnished a partial antidote to its enervating tendency. It made the brother and sister highly enthusiastic, but it did not entirely substitute romance for reality. They knew very little of the world, yet the castles which they built in the air, were of brick and mortar, not of crystal and vapour. The plan which Randolph disclosed to his dying father, had been often discussed between himself and Helen. An old edition of Blackstone's Commentaries, and one, equally out of date of Burn's Justice, which he found in the library, attested by their wear and tear, the diligence of the young student, who little thought of the depth to which he must dive, to find the sands of the legal Pactolus. To go to London, to take some suburban lodging, to dwell in frugal retirement, was the scheme arranged by Randolph and Helen *Morton*. Mr. Griffith and Polydore would be their only confidants; the former would introduce Randolph to the family lawyer, of course in his feigned name, who would procure his admission at an Inn of Court; five years—that was the bitter in the cup—five long years would qualify him for the bar: and then, he should stretch forth his hand and collect the golden grains. When a sufficiency of the commodity was stored up, Randolph and Helen *Trevethlan* would arrive one fine day at Trevethlan Castle, which would have been gradually restored to receive them, and there would be ringing of bells and firing of cannon; a new flag would fly from the lofty watch-tower; Griffith and his wife would weep for joy; Polydore would give them his blessing; and the sun of Trevethlan, long hidden by clouds, would shine out with a glory never to be again obscured.

These visions were interrupted by Mr. Trevethlan's illness and death. The preparations necessary for the funeral devolved upon the steward and his wife. Mrs. Griffith produced some velvet which had once been black, wherewith to hang the state chamber, and a few tapers lighted up the solemn mockery. The orphan brother and sister sat afar in those rooms, which have been already described as overlooking a small flower garden. The blinds, lowered reverentially, debarred the occupants from beholding the prospect, and seemed to sever them from all communion with the world. They leant against each other in sad silence, as if they were too feeble to sustain themselves apart, and required mutual support. Little had they thought how much the loss, even of their father, could add to the loneliness of Trevethlan Castle. And the scheme on which they had so long and so often dwelt in Merlin's Cave, and which then seemed so simple and feasible, now assumed a hard and perplexing aspect. The edifice, which at a distance looked fair and stately, presented on a nearer view the whited wall of the sepulchre.

Wrapped in such reverie, with their arms twined around each other, they were sitting side by side, the day preceding that appointed for the funeral, when the chaplain entered with a letter in his hand. Very rare, indeed, was the arrival of such a missive at the castle, and Polydore's appearance roused the mourners from their lethargy. He delivered the epistle to Randolph, and retired with delicate kindness. It was dated from May Fair, London, and was to the following effect:—

"MY DEAR NEPHEW,

"The estrangement, which has so long and so unhappily divided our families, cannot deter me from offering you and my niece, the sincere condolence both of Mrs. Trevethlan Pendarrel and of myself, on the recent melancholy event.

"Most deeply do I regret that a pressure of engagements will prevent me from attending the last obsequies of my lamented relative; but Mrs. Trevethlan Pendarrel intends to have the pleasure of calling at Trevethlan Castle before many days have elapsed, and of making the acquaintance of her nephew and niece.

"Fearing that circumstances may render the funeral an embarrassment, and awaiting a satisfactory arrangement for the comfort of yourself and your sister, I have ventured to direct my bankers, Messrs.———, to honour the drafts of Mr. Randolph Trevethlan to the amount of £500.

"Mrs. Trevethlan Pendarrel unites in the regard with which

"I am,

"My dear nephew,

"Yours very affectionately,

"P. TREVETHLAN PENDARREL."

Helen watched her brother's face as he read this effusion of sympathy, and was almost alarmed at the change which came over it. He held the letter at arm's length, and gazed upon it: the lessons of the portrait-gallery crowded thickly upon him, and those of the library were forgotten.

"May I read it, Randolph?" his sister asked, timidly laying her hand on his extended arm.

"Read it!" he repeated. "Ay, read it, Helen; read it, and learn what we have become! Well might our father say that a favour received from Philip Pendarrel would disturb him in his grave."

"Was it not kindly meant?" Helen said, gently, after perusing the letter.

"Is insult ever kind?" asked her brother in reply. "Think they the spirit of our house is extinct, that they come in such hot haste to exult over its decay? Helen, the letter gives me heart. Why have we desponded of our scheme? We are not yet absolutely beggars. The last moveable in the castle shall be sold, the last farthing spent, in the struggle for independence. And if it fail, we will come back to our cold hearth, and here, for the last time, our hearts shall beat together as they do now. But, Helen, my dearest sister, we will not fail."

"And this promised visit?" his sister said, after a pause.

"Mrs. Pendarrel must return as she comes," said Randolph. "She does not cross the threshold of Trevethlan Castle while I am its master.—Come, let us take a turn in the gallery."

Helen sighed as she took her brother's arm for the walk he proposed. The conflict which restored his spirit, saddened hers. It seemed a presage of evil, that the first step of the orphans should involve them in a quarrel with their nearest relations. The rowan bends wailing under the breeze which the oak defies. Several times had the length of the gallery been traversed in silence, when Randolph produced a small miniature, and showed it to his sister.

"See, Helen," he said: "they found this upon him. I imagine it is her likeness—Mrs. Pendarrel's."

"It is very beautiful," Helen remarked.

"Very beautiful," repeated her brother, "at first sight. But is it not a beauty rather to fear than to love? There is strong expression in the face—but of what? Is hatred or affection most apparent in those inscrutable dark eyes? Is it good-humour or disdain that curls those lips?"

"And why," Helen asked, "do you think it is a portrait of Mrs. Pendarrel?"

"Because, my dear sister, our poor father told me she was once very dear to him: she encouraged him, he said, and refused him. When they brought me this picture, it recalled his words. There is a key to the history which we have dimly heard."

Again the orphans made several turns in the gallery, musing in silence. Then Randolph spoke:—

"Yes, Helen!—that was the beauty destined to be the ruin of our house. In each successive crash that broke upon his head, our father hoped to find forgetfulness of the past. But it was too deeply written on his heart. And when the desolation was complete, he came back here to hide anguish under pride, to cover tenderness with stern reserve. Hence that cold demeanour which kept even his children at a distance, and, seeming to reject their affection, checked, but did not stifle, its growth. The story has made him more dear to me than ever before. And now she, who broke his heart and drove him to ruin, insults us with her sympathy and her wealth."

"She must herself be old," said Helen. "Perhaps she, too, has had sorrows. I would fain believe you misinterpret that letter."

"Your wish is what it should be," observed Randolph: "I should be glad to think it well founded. Forgive me, dear sister, if, for once, I differ from you. We must not see Mrs. Pendarrel."

The next day Randolph Trevethlan followed his father's remains to the vault in the village churchyard. It was but a short space from the gates of the base-court, and within the precinct still appertaining to the castle. Polydore Riches performed the funeral rites, and the grave closed over the dead.

The chief mourner had been too much absorbed in his own emotions during the ceremony to notice the bystanders; but when it was over, he looked round to thank such as were known to him, for their sympathy and respect. While so engaged, he happened to turn his eye on a couple, who stood a little apart, beneath the shade of an old yew tree. They were a young man about his own age, and a decrepit old woman. They returned his look with an air which might be termed insolent, and which, under other circumstances, might have provoked his anger. But the features of the youth, although coarse and sinister, seemed vaguely to resemble some with which Randolph was familiar, and as he gazed upon them, he asked the chaplain if he knew who the stranger was. Before Polydore could reply, the old woman answered, having seen, not heard, the question.

"Who am I? Thy mother's mother: thy grandmother. Who is this? Thy mother's sister's son: thy cousin. We were not asked to the burying, but we came. To weep for a son-in-law? To weep for an uncle? Did he weep for his wife? Na, na."

Randolph was inexpressibly shocked.

"I dreamt not of this," he said to the chaplain in a low tone. "Something must be done. Are they in distress?"

"Na, na," said the old woman with a frightful grin, again interpreting the motion of his lips, "we want nothing of you, Mr. Randolph Trevethlan. We belong to Pendar'l now. And so will Trevethlan.

'When the castle a bride from the cot shall claim,Pendar'l and Trevethlan shall own one name.'

Margaret Basset's mother seeks not from a son the help which a husband refused."

Polydore put his arm through Randolph's, and drew him away. The late Mr. Trevethlan's marriage had been a prohibited subject at the castle, and all that his children knew concerning it, was, that their mother had been of humble birth. So this was his son's first introduction to his maternal relations. "It is thus," thought the chaplain, "that the sins of the fathers are visited upon the children."

The resemblance which Randolph had detected in the young man's features, was to himself. It was of that vague character which the eye often discovers in an unknown portrait, depending not on complexion, or lineaments, or even expression, and difficult, therefore, to make visible to another's perception. So now a third person would probably have failed to see the likeness, recognised at once by the heir of Trevethlan. For while candour and courage distinguished Randolph's countenance, cunning and meanness lurked in the aspect of Michael Sinson.

The development of such traits in the peasant might be owing to his early life. When Margaret Basset sorrowfully obeyed the order which seemed to make her mistress of Trevethlan Castle, her family conceived great hopes from her elevation, instead of sympathising in her grief. Her nephew, Michael, was trained in the habits they fancied most likely to conciliate the favour of their lord, vulgar obsequiousness and fawning dissimulation. For some time after Mrs. Trevethlan's death, he was allowed to hang about the castle, enjoying the benefit of Polydore's instruction, and encouraged in the idea, that he might grow to be the confidant and companion of the youthful heir. Those who thought so, little knew Mr. Trevethlan. Pride hates the sycophancy which is acceptable to vanity. He was simply disgusted by the offered homage; and at once perceiving its drift, excluded his wife's relations from all connexion with his household, and ejected them from their little farm. They settled upon the neighbouring estates of Pendarrel, cherishing a natural enmity against their late landlord, and beholding his ruin with a certain exultation. They also chose to consider that poor Margaret had been aggrieved by the compulsion in which they themselves participated, and thus sharpened craft and malice with the feeling of injury. With such spiteful mind old Maud Basset came to the funeral, and flung in Randolph's teeth a prophecy, which had been much recited of late years among the peasantry of the neighbourhood.

And now Trevethlan Castle re-assumed its usual appearance. One of Randolph's first cares after the funeral was to warn Jeffrey, the porter, that all visitors whatsoever who might present themselves at the gates, were to be informed neither he nor his sister was at home, and were not to be admitted on any pretence. Archbishop Secker is reported to have said, that the *first* person who used this excuse told a lie. It sorely puzzled old Jeffrey's notions of morality.

"Not at home, Master Randolph," he said; "and are ye and my young lady to leave us so soon?"

"No, Jeffrey," was the answer; "we are not going away immediately. But we desire to see no company, and this is the usual mode of saying so."

"Good truth, Master Randolph, 'twill be a strange thing for company to come to Trevethlan," said the porter. "And where shall I say you are gone?"

"Nowhere," replied Randolph. "Say no more than that we are not at home; and do not open the gates, whoever may ask."

"Trust old Jeffrey to obey a Trevethlan," the retainer said as his master retired; "and faith, we want no fine folks here spying out the nakedness of the land. Jeffrey will send them away with a flea in their ear."

CHAPTER III.

"Nature never framed a woman's heart
Of prouder stuff than that of Beatrice:
Disdain and scorn ride sparkling in her eyes,
Misprising what they look on; and her wit
Values itself so highly, that to her
All matter else seems weak."

SHAKSPEARE.

The gentleman so addressed put down an untasted glass of wine with which he was about to give zest to his luncheon, and he looked towards the lady who spoke. She was reading a newspaper.

"Did you observe this?" she continued. "We regret to announce the death of Henry Trevethlan, Esq., of Trevethlan Castle!"

"My poor nephew!" exclaimed the gentleman.

The lady flung a glance upon him, which made him lower his eyes, and read on. "He is succeeded in his estates—his estates!—by his son Randolph Trevethlan, Esq., who, with his sister, is now at the castle."

Mr. Pendarrel, probably thinking of the look which had just rebuked him, made no further observation.

"Have you nothing to remark upon this intelligence?" asked his wife. "No commiseration for your great nephew and niece, as well as their father?"

"They must be very poor," her husband answered. "Anything I can do—"

"Anything you can do, Mr. Trevethlan Pendarrel!" the lady exclaimed, interrupting him sharply. "You must buy me the castle, and they may live on the price.

'Pendar'l and Trevethlan shall own one name!'"

She laid aside the newspaper, and rising, walked to and fro in the apartment, speaking in a tone free from the irony and scorn which had given an unfeminine expression to her previous words.

"Let me see. Seventeen, ninety-six-seven—Randolph must be just of age. And Helen a year or two younger. Poor! Indeed they must be poor. The castle will be very ornamental as a ruin. Already it is more picturesque than habitable. They will be relieved to have it taken off their hands. And we can be generous. If not, what do they know? Why, Randolph has never slept away. They must be as wild as mountain-goats. And their society! What ideas can they have formed of life? Yet we may be generous; if they like, friendly.

There is a pleasant cottage on the shore under Pendarrel: comfortable; suitable for straitened means; in wild scenery, like Trevethlan. They might have it at an easy rent; or in part purchase of the castle."

Thus, Alnaschar-like, Mrs. Pendarrel accomplished in reverie what had long been the settled purpose of her mind. Such was the vision that rose from her basket of crockery. She was a woman of genius, and knew it, and loved the knowledge.

"Mr. Trevethlan Pendarrel, have you yet finished your luncheon? Then follow me to the library. You must write to Randolph; and I shall go down to Cornwall next week, and visit him and his sister."

In the library the lady dictated the letter which the reader has already perused. When her husband looked over what he had written, he ventured to remonstrate.

"Do you not think, my dear Esther, this is rather, just a little, the least in the world; you know what I mean."

"No, I do not, Mr. Trevethlan Pendarrel. I am not initiated in the mysteries of your office, where they use language to conceal their thoughts."

"Nay, I know it is not your intention," continued her husband; "but might it not be supposed? It would be quite wrong, of course. Still, perhaps, they might think—people do form such curious ideas."

"Your ideas seem very curious indeed," said the lady. "What on earth do you mean?"

"Why, my dear Esther, might not this letter, quite undesignedly, quite— might it not wound Mr. Randolph Trevethlan's feelings?"

"Not if I appreciate them rightly, Mr. Trevethlan Pendarrel," answered his wife; "and it will furnish me with a key to his character. If, as I fully expect, that offer is regarded as kind, and gratefully accepted, the heir of Trevethlan becomes my humble dependent. If, as I think very unlikely, the letter is resented as an affront, then I know that the old spirit still animates the old ruin, and I prepare accordingly. Is it sealed? Well: remember to give the instruction to Messrs——."

And so saying, the lady withdrew. Her husband was the brother of the late Henry Trevethlan's father, and, therefore, great-uncle to Randolph; but having been born more than twenty years after his elder brother, he was but little older than his nephew, and was brought up in companionship with him at Trevethlan Castle. Rivalry for the hand of Esther Pendarrel disturbed their affection soon after Henry succeeded to the estates, and it gave place to hatred, when Philip carried off the prize and assumed his wife's name.

Rumour said, that nothing but Henry's positive refusal to submit to this condition, led to his rejection.

For once rumour was probably right. The families of Trevethlan and Pendarrel had long lived in the usual friendship of neighbours, frequently intermarrying, but never united under one head. When, however, circumstances made Esther sole heiress of her house, it seemed likely that this might at last occur, and that the name of Pendarrel might merge in that of Trevethlan. The lady's own attention was attracted to this contingency by a little altercation she happened to overhear between two peasants, respecting the prophecy already quoted.

"Well, Jem," said one, "ye see Pendar'l's like to come to Trevethlan without a bride from under the thatch. 'T is a bonny lady whereby they'll own one name."

"Do not ye think it, Robin," answered the other. "The saying's as old as Carn Dew. My lady's not one to sink her name: there's that in her eye tells another tale."

When Esther heard these remarks, the first rustic seemed to be much nearer the truth than the second; for Henry Trevethlan was so close an attendant upon her, that it could not be supposed that his assiduity was unwelcome. But she had been trained in a sufficiently high sense of her own importance; and the peasant's words made her ponder, and roused the pride which had almost been laid to sleep by love. She quarrelled with Henry, and married Philip.

Her first lover endeavoured to forget his disappointment in the excitement of play. She, always hoping to realize the prediction in her own sense, rejoiced in adding the estates which he sold, one after another, to the already extensive domains of Pendarrel. By degrees, she thus drove the enemy into his citadel, and beleaguered him on all sides, trusting at last to starve him into submission. And now that the defence had fallen into young and inexperienced hands, she rushed eagerly to the assault, heralding it with the demand for a capitulation, contained in the letter she caused her husband to write.

He, poor man, did not count for much in his wife's arrangements. At home, he was nearly a nonentity; abroad, he held a subordinate place of some importance under Government. His official consequence consoled him for his domestic insignificance; and some such comfort he needed; for he had no will of his own whenever Esther interfered, so rigorous was the sway wherewith the strong mind ruled the weak.

Their family—a sore point was this with Mrs. Pendarrel, who foresaw that in some shape her own manœuvre must be repeated—consisted of two daughters, Gertrude and Mildred. Gertrude was nearly thirty, married, but without offspring: Mildred was not quite twenty. In appearance, they both resembled their mother, and might be imagined to exhibit traces of the ancient people said, in some legends, to have founded Marazion.

Esther lost no time in fulfilling her purpose of visiting the orphans. As soon as possible after the despatch of the letter, she started for Pendarrel Hall, which, unlike Trevethlan Castle, was a modern mansion, surrounded by a large park. The day after her arrival, she drove to perform her errand.

Old Jeffrey had pondered much on the novel instructions received from his young master; and every sound of the gate-bell roused him to a great display of vigilance. First, he reconnoitred the party seeking admission, through a loop-hole: if that scrutiny were satisfactory, he opened a slit in the wicket, and held a parley: if this proved equally free from danger, he unclosed the wicket itself, and allowed the visitor to enter. Hitherto, he had not been called upon to pronounce the message of exclusion.

But the sound of an approaching carriage awoke all the caution of the old warder. Mrs. Pendarrel's chariot wound heavily up the now rugged road, which led through the base-court to the main gateway of the castle. The lady looked from side to side, and viewed the surrounding desolation with some secret triumph, as betokening a necessity which must be glad to accept relief. At length her carriage drew up in front of the arched portal, and a servant alighted, and rang the bell with correct violence.

Old Jeffrey had sufficient shrewdness to know that such an attack as this could not be repelled from the loop-hole; so he descended to parley through the opening in the wicket.

"Now, sir," said the invading servant, "how long is my lady to wait?"

"Who did you want to see?" asked the porter in turn.

"Open the gates, sir: let us drive to the hall-door."

"Troth," said Jeffrey, "this is the hall-door just now. Who did ye want to see?"

Mrs. Pendarrel, slightly impatient, repeated her servant's demand from the window of the carriage: Jeffrey met it with the same question.

"Mr. Trevethlan," said the lady.

"Mr. Trevethlan's not at home," said the obstinate warder.

"Not at home, sir! What do you mean? Where is he?"

"He's not at home," Jeffrey repeated.

Mrs. Pendarrel mused for a moment.

"Miss Trevethlan is at home, I suppose?" she asked.

"Miss Trevethlan is not at home," was again the reply.

"This is insolence," the lady said. "Do you know, sir, who I am?"

"I think I know the Pendar'l liveries," answered Jeffrey.

"Home," said Mrs. Pendarrel to her servant. And the carriage rattled down the descent.

A young man was leaning on the gate of the base-court: as the chariot approached, he opened it, and stood cap in hand while the lady drove through. She pulled the check-string, and beckoned the stranger to the window.

"Do you belong to the castle?" she asked, when he drew near.

"No, in good truth, ma'am," the youth replied with a peculiar smile: "I am a tenant of Pendar'l."

"What is your name?"

"Sinson, ma'am; Michael Sinson at your service, ma'am; grandson of old Maud Basset."

"What!" exclaimed the lady hastily, "a relation——"

"The late Mrs. Trevethlan's nephew, ma'am," said Michael.

"Come to the hall to-morrow," Mrs. Pendarrel said; "I may be able to employ you."

Michael made a cringing bow, and the carriage drove on.

"So," mused its occupant, "it is war. The old spirit does animate the old ruin. A pleasant pastime, Henry Trevethlan, have you bequeathed to your children. Long shall your race rue the day, when you took a woman at her first word. Was not Esther Pendarrel worth asking twice? Was it impossible to conciliate her pride, except by the sacrifice of your own? Was no allowance to be made for the petulance of a girl nursed by flattery? Was there no middle course? Might not Trevethlan have been preserved, yet Pendarrel not extinguished? I smiled when you left me: I smiled when I saw your rapid gallop down the avenue: I smiled still, when I heard you were departed to London. No falconer's voice, methought, will be required, 'to lure my tassel-gentle back again.' A week—and another, and another—and no news. A month, and news. His kinsman comes. To intercede for him? Ah, no. To tell me of his folly, and to plead for himself. 'There is no fury like a woman scorned.' I listened, but it was long before I consented. A bold wooer truly was my worthy lord! Did he not venture to urge, that his nephew's passion was so ardent, it would prevent him from any other union? That therefore the castle would descend to him? That so the properties would be united in my name? That he loved me more—oh, cant and hypocrisy, how I loathed you at the time! Yet I listened, and listened, and in my wrath and for my sorrow, consented. Did I drive you to ruin, Henry Trevethlan? Did I embitter your days? Alas! mine have been equally dark. Proud man, I ask again, why did you trample on me? Why might we not minister to our mutual happiness, instead of running a race for revenge? I could not, you knew I could not, unasked, revoke my words. Might I not have had the opportunity? And should I submit to my doom in patience?

"And you have bequeathed your hatred to your children. To the children of Margaret Basset. And, verily, they seem worthy of the trust. But they shall find their match in Esther Pendarrel. And now the plan of the campaign. I must learn the nature of the ground. Then, sound trumpets, and no quarter."

The following morning young Sinson fulfilled Mrs. Pendarrel's behest, by calling at the hall, where he had an interview of some length with its mistress. One of the park lodges, Wilderness gate, happened to be vacant at the time, and was assigned to Michael as a residence, in consideration of services, either past or to come, which were a mystery to the retainers of the family, among whom some jealousy was created by the preference.

Within a few days afterwards, Mrs. Pendarrel returned to London.

CHAPTER IV.

"But can the noble mind for ever brood,
The willing victim of a weary mood,
On heartless cares that squander life away,
And cloud young genius brightening into day?
 Shame to the coward thought that e'er betrayed
The noon of manhood to a myrtle shade!"

CAMPBELL.

The Trevethlans, it has already been remarked, were a crotchetty race. One of their peculiarities was displayed in the disposition of their property. No portion had been entailed within the memory of man, and the whole had very frequently descended simply by inheritance. Wills were of rare occurrence among the family muniments, and marked the existence of disagreement. And now that cause was active, and produced its effect. A few days after Mr. Trevethlan's funeral, his children were summoned by the chaplain to hear the last desires of their parent, Mr. Griffith being also present with his account books.

The will which Polydore produced was very short and simple. The testator merely appointed the Rev. Polydore Riches and Mr. Edward Griffith, to be the guardians of his children, in case he died before they were of age, leaving his property to descend by inheritance. A short silence ensued when the chaplain finished reading the document: it was first broken by the steward.

"It is but a small patrimony," he said, "Mr. Trevethlan, that you inherit. A very small patrimony for the owner of this castle. And a sad trust is this for me, who can remember, when from the top of the watch-tower, we saw little that was not ours."

"Mr. Griffith," Randolph said, "we must think of the present and the future, not of the past. But if the trust is unwelcome, do not undertake it."

"The trust is not unwelcome, Randolph," observed the chaplain, with a slight accent of reproof. "The sadness of which our friend speaks is caused by the lightness, not the oppressiveness, of our duty. We promised to undertake it, and we shall feel pleasure in fulfilling it, so as most effectually to promote your welfare in every respect."

"I know it," said the heir. "I am sure of it; I did not mean to doubt Mr. Griffith's good will."

"Here," the steward said, opening one of his books, "here are the accounts of the last few years: and here is an abstract or estimate, which I have prepared from them, showing the probable receipts and the necessary expenses for the future."

Randolph took the paper from Mr. Griffith's hands, and perused it attentively, his sister also looking over him.

"From this," he said at length, "I perceive that our total income is something under seven hundred pounds a year, and the needful outgoings something more than two; leaving us a clear revenue of four hundred. Why, Helen, we are rich!"

"They are young," the steward observed aside to Polydore.

The brother and sister conferred together for a few minutes in an under tone. Then Randolph spoke aloud:—

"Mr. Riches, the expenditure of the castle household, as here set down, is very small. Surely it does not include—" He stopped.

"I know what you would say, Randolph," the chaplain remarked. "The services of Mr. Griffith and myself have already been remunerated far in advance. There is nothing due on our account, nor will there be for a long time."

Metaphorically, this might be true. Randolph looked incredulous.

"Mr. Trevethlan," said the steward, "I hope you will not press us into a difficulty. That statement is made up strictly from my books; and unless you desire to alter the establishment——"

"Oh, no, certainly not," Randolph exclaimed. "I wish everything to go on as hitherto."

"And have you formed any plan for the future?" the chaplain asked. "Do you propose to live here in retirement, or to go into the world?"

This question was not answered immediately. Randolph's heart was full. He rose from his seat and walked to a window of the apartment, where he leant his forehead against the glass, and gazed upon the sea. A mist clouded his eyes. Helen came softly to his side, and laid her hand on his shoulder, but he turned not towards her, for it was of her loneliness that he was thinking.

"'Tis a hard question for him, Mr. Riches," said Griffith.

"He will answer it as he ought," observed the chaplain.

"Randolph," Helen whispered in the mean time, "is this our firmness? Who said, 'we will not fail?' See, it is my turn now."

He turned and looked at her, meeting a smile so full of hope, that his momentary irresolution vanished at once. The castle rose again in the air, firm and substantial. He led his sister back to her seat, and resuming his own, said:—

"You, Mr. Riches, and you, my good sir, will not smile at a scheme which has been often discussed by my sister and myself, and to which our poor father assented almost with his parting words. If we are visionaries, you will be gentle in removing the illusion. This then is our plan."

And at some length, Randolph unfolded the design with which the reader is already acquainted. Both the chaplain and the steward listened with great interest, although the latter could not avoid smiling to himself, as he perceived the little artifices by which the speaker blinded his eyes to the difficulties of his proposition. Polydore was willing to be also blind to them.

"And now, my friends," Randolph concluded, having talked himself into cheerfulness, "we will leave you to deliberate on our romance. Helen and I will go to the flower-garden, and await the reply of the oracle. Let it be at least decisive."

So saying, he took Helen's arm upon his, and led her from the room. Griffith looked at the chaplain, and repeated his previous observation, "they are young."

"Youth and imprudence are not necessarily connected, Mr. Griffith," answered Polydore.

"And are you disposed to sanction this scheme?" the steward asked. "Do not you see its difficulties? Are fortunes to be found now as in nursery tales? And at the bar, of all ways? Even in my narrow experience, what failures have I known! and with fairer prospects than Mr. Randolph's. It is a lottery, Mr. Riches; a mere lottery."

"It is not the chance of a prize," said the chaplain, "upon which I reckon. I hate lotteries. It is the price which must in this instance be paid for a chance, and which I believe Randolph is prepared to pay, that reconciles me to the speculation."

"You mean the labour bestowed and the knowledge acquired," observed Griffith. "Is it of the best kind? Might not better be obtained here?"

"You interpret my meaning rightly but not completely, Mr. Griffith," the chaplain said. "I include in the term knowledge, knowledge of the world; that knowledge, without which we cannot love the world. A recluse may fancy that he loves his race, but it is not until he has actually felt their kindness, ay, and their unkindness, that he can realize the affection. A man is worthless until he has experienced some of the buffeting of the world."

"And do you think Mr. Randolph qualified to withstand it to advantage?" the steward inquired.

"Do I, Mr. Griffith?" exclaimed Polydore. "I should take shame to myself if I did not. He may not succeed at the bar. He may return to Trevethlan Castle as poor as he quits it. As poor, I mean, in worldly goods. But he will return to enjoy life: not to mope away a miserable time of idleness amongst these gray walls: not to pine for what is unattainable, and sicken with ever-increasing discontent: not to vanish from the stage an unprofitable supernumerary. No, the habits he will have acquired will accompany him in his retreat; in his solitude he will still be active; he will give his thoughts to the world; he will be a benefactor to his race. Let him go, Mr. Griffith. The very chivalry of the idea is charming in my eyes. Believe me, his portrait will one day be an honour to our gallery."

The steward was infected with Polydore's enthusiasm. He shook the chaplain's hand with great warmth.

"Mr. Riches," he said, "I know how much Trevethlan owes to you; and your words inspire me with hope. Yet, Miss Helen, is the scheme equally adapted for her?"

"And why not, my good sir?" answered the chaplain. "Where can she be better than with her brother? What can cheer his studies, no trifle, Mr. Griffith, like her company when they are over? What would not I have given for a sister to make my tea at college? She will be his comfort and his stay; his light and his hope; his joy and his pride. Let them go, my friend; we shall see a dance at Trevethlan yet."

Griffith, a quiet and thoughtful man, was entirely carried away by the increasing animation of the chaplain. In silence he assented to Polydore's conclusion. "Come," said the latter, "let us seek them in their garden;" and he took the steward's arm and led him thither. On their way prudential considerations again beset the man of business, and he stopped the man of letters to speak of their wards' inexperience.

"Inexperience!" echoed the divine; "and how shall they gain experience? Staying here, they will always be inexperienced. No fear, my friend; give them a good introduction to Winter, and they'll do. Winter's the very personification of prudence."

Randolph and his sister were watching the bees on a bed of mignionette, one of the pleasantest pastimes afforded by a garden in autumn. The eye is gratified by the unceasing flutter of the busy insects; the ear rejoices in the perpetual murmur accompanying their industry; a delicious fragrance arises from the gently agitated florets; and some observers may, perhaps, remember a moral they were taught to lisp in childhood, and cast a fond retrospect over their early years.

"Joy for you, Randolph Morton," cried the chaplain; "and for you, Helen Morton; joy for your old master, and for the towers of Trevethlan. You shall go forth like Fortunio, without needing his seven servants; like Fortunatus, without requiring his purse."

In his glee Polydore had quitted Mr. Griffith, and preceded him. The brother and sister turned at the sound of his voice, ran rather than walked to meet him, and each seizing a hand, as they used of old, looked into his face with sparkling eyes.

"Be still," he said, "be still, or Mr. Griffith will declare you must not be trusted alone."

"And may we go?" Randolph asked. "May I try to be useful upon earth?"

"Stay away, Mr. Griffith," cried the chaplain to the steward, who was now approaching; "stay away, or you will say that even I am a child. Yes," he continued, turning to Randolph, "yes, you shall have your wish, and we doubt not that with the blessing of God, you will prosper to your heart's content."

Warm and sincere were the acknowledgments paid by the orphans to their guardians for this acquiescence in their scheme; and by Polydore, at least, they were as warmly returned. Child-like, but not childish, was the good chaplain in his affections. And if the sanguine ardour of youth is a glorious thing, surely the tempered enthusiasm of mature age is as admirable, and less uncertain.

The preparations for departure were commenced immediately. Mrs. Griffith was saddened a little when Helen brought her the news; but she recovered her spirits under the influence of her old pupil's animation. And strange it would have been, if the anticipation of so great a change had not produced considerable excitement in those upon whom it was about to fall. They had never—as Mrs. Pendarrel remarked—spent a night away from the castle; they had seen no town larger than Penzance; they had been familiar with none save the household around them. Wonderful it would have been, if with a calm pulse they could contemplate abiding in mighty London, among a host of strangers, and competing in the great race of life. Yet upon their earnest tempers the prospect produced less effect than it would on dispositions less serious; and they watched and superintended the necessary arrangements with a foresight which delighted Polydore, and was satisfactory even to the steward.

At length, these were completed, and the eve of the journey arrived. The autumnal sun was setting in radiance over the opposite side of Mount's Bay, when the orphans, moved by a sympathetic impulse, took their way for a farewell visit to Merlin's Cave. A purple flush lay on the uplands above Gulvall and Ludgvan; there was scarce a ripple on the sea, and the fishermen of Newlyn were obliged to use their oars to gain the offing. The tranquillity of the evening sank into the hearts of the brother and sister, as they sat in silence, side by side, under their little canopy of rock. But at last, Helen interrupted the reverie. The sun had reached the crest of the hills; the tower of St. Paul's Church stood out dark against the sky, with its edges fringed by the level rays; the flush on the heather had grown deeper and warmer; when she suddenly began to sing, to an old Jacobite air, a ballad, composed by an ancestor who fled to Switzerland at the Restoration, and known in the family as "Trevethlan's Farewell:"—

"Farewell to Trevethlan! A farewell for ever!
Farewell to the towers that stand by the sea!
Ah! hard is my fortune from home so to sever,
And seek me a shelter where still men are free!

"No more at midsummer to see our hills lighted
With bonfires that welcome the eve of St. John;
No more by old Christmas to frolic invited,
To greet our fair orchards with glad benison;—

"Nor yet in the May-time, at Helston's gay furry,
With garlands of oak-leaves to dance to the song;
But far o'er the waters an exile to hurry,
And pine for my kinsmen strange faces among.

"Ay, sad as the children of Morvah retreating
To Pendeen's dark caverns beside the sea-swell,
While the crags of Penvonlas bewailed the fierce meeting,
And Mên Skryfa marked where Rialobran fell.

"The sun will still brighten St. Michael's high tower,
And redden at setting the rocks of Trereen;
The billow lave gently Lamorna's soft bower,
By banished Trevethlan no more to be seen.

"The maidens of Madron will hie to their fountain,
And drop the smooth pebble his fortune to tell—
Ah! glad for the exile, afar on the mountain,
The day when no ripple shall ruffle the well.

"But, hark! 'tis the signal from home now to sever—O'er ruin Tregagel is howling his glee:Farewell to Trevethlan! A farewell for ever!Farewell to the towers that stand by the sea!"

The last note of Helen's song had some time died away, and the sun had sunk behind the hill; but the western sky was still ruddy, and the warm tint still lingered on the moorlands.

"Surely, my dear sister," Randolph said, with a gentle smile, "your song is not of good omen for our exile."

"Oh! yes," Helen answered quickly; "recollect that Reginald survived the Revolution, and ended his days happily at Trevethlan."

"'T was a long banishment, Helen," observed her brother. "But the sun has set. Let us return to the castle."

And, making not a few pauses, they pursued the path homewards.

CHAPTER V.

"Then hope grew round me like the twining vine,
And fruits and foliage, not my own, seemed mine."

COLERIDGE.

The promise of the red evening described in the last chapter was faithfully kept, and a splendid day witnessed the departure of the heir of Trevethlan and his sister from their ancestral home. At their earnest request, Polydore Riches accompanied them as far as Falmouth, from whence places had been secured for London by the mail. The chaplain thought that the more sudden the change, the better it would be borne; and would gladly at once have cast the orphans upon their own resources; but he succumbed to their entreaties. And if a tear glistened in Polydore's eye when the mail had disappeared round the first corner, it surely will not be thought to bring discredit upon his head.

In subdued sadness the chaplain returned to the castle. There it was generally understood that Mr. Randolph and Miss Helen were going to travel abroad for some years. And this impression was confirmed by the following announcement, which appeared in the local journals, and was copied into some of the metropolitan:—"We are informed that Mr. and Miss Trevethlan have left Trevethlan Castle, to make a sojourn of some duration in the South of Europe." The paragraph flavoured many a cup of tea at Helston and Penzance, and attracted attention at one house in May Fair.

But the mail is rattling along, to the music of the guard's horn and the quadrupedant sound of the horses, heedless alike of local verjuice and of London pride. Not yet had it been polished into the dashing Quicksilver, but it rattled along very respectably, contented with itself, and despising the heavy Subscription. Poor thing!—its vanity has been severely punished. Needless it is to dwell on the incidents of the journey. Long and wearisome it was, and glad were the orphans when the wheels had made their last turn, and they alighted about daybreak in the yard of the old Bull and Mouth, St. Martin's-le-Grand. Slumber soon brought oblivion both of care and fatigue.

When Randolph, leaving his chamber near noon, was shown into a sitting-room, he found Helen already there. She was looking out of the old-fashioned window, the heavy wood-work of which might remind her of farm-houses in her own country. Traffic was in full vigour in the street below, and the noise and hurry so confused her, that she was not aware of her brother's approach until he stood by her side.

"Welcome to London, Miss Helen Morton," he said, becoming in turn amazed at the scene beneath his eyes.

They breakfasted with considerable gaiety in the excitement of their new situation; and then Randolph started to discover Mr. Winter's offices in Lincoln's Inn; while his sister sat down to write Polydore an account of their safe arrival at their journey's end.

Griffith had already written to the attorney, requesting his services on behalf of the son of an old friend, recently deceased. Mr. Morton, he said, possessed a small competence, and was desirous of proceeding to the bar. He would be in town with his only sister in a few days, and any kindness which Mr. Winter could show them would confer a great favour upon his correspondent.

Winter has been spoken of by the chaplain as an impersonation of prudence. The description was just; but it was a prudence untainted by the slightest selfishness. He was a man of a large, liberal, and honourable nature, without a trace of the narrow-mindedness so often and so erroneously thought inseparable from his profession; he was so genial, withal, in his temper, that his friends used to quote him as a notable example of the rule, that surnames go by contraries. Spring, they would say, was the proper season for Winter, and Winter was proper for all seasons. Happy were they, privileged in July to sip his claret in the arbour of his garden at Hampstead—there was a touch of the Cockney about him—and in December to quaff his old port in his sanctum within-doors: hours never grudged by Mrs. Winter, who was as cheerful as her spouse.

For several generations the legal business of the Trevethlan family had been managed in the office over which Mr. Winter now presided; and it was with a sad heart that the worthy attorney effected the alienations ordered by the late owner of the castle. He entertained a high regard for the steward, and was quite prepared to extend it to the son of his friend. No time elapsed after Randolph had sent in his name, before he was ushered into Mr. Winter's private room.

"Welcome, my young friend," the lawyer cried, extending his hand, and looking with satisfaction on Randolph's open countenance, "welcome to town. I have been expecting you: it is a pleasure to know a friend of Griffith's. How is the worthy steward? He has had his trials, poor man! Trevethlan is not what it was—Ah me! The young squire going abroad, I understand. No use. He should marry, Mr. Morton. There's many a girl would jump at the castle, even yet.—So you are for the bar. A fashionable profession just now, Mr. Morton. Red coats are cheap. Cornets from Waterloo—midshipmen of Trafalgar—all rushing to the law. Uncommonly martial it is just now. *N'importe*: there's room for all. But this by-and-by.—Miss Morton came with you—Where have you left her?—Not over-fatigued, I hope?"

The attorney's volubility was meant to give his new acquaintance time to overcome his first diffidence, and effected its object. Randolph thanked him, and gave the information asked for.

"Lodgings," said Winter, "that's what you want, I suppose? There is a friend of mine on Hampstead Heath, who might perhaps suit you. An old clerk in one of the great city houses, and a sterling fellow; with an amiable old maiden sister. Would you like to try it?"

"Surely, my dear sir," Randolph answered.

"I thought so," Winter said. "Then just observe: here is the precise address. A porter of the inn will put you and Miss Morton into a coach, which will drop you at Peach's door. Tell Clotilda, Miss Peach, I mean, you are from me. If you like it, well. Let Miss Morton take possession then and there. You come back for the luggage. If it does not suit, ask Miss Peach the way to my house—I live at Hampstead—leave your sister there, and equally come back for the traps. I shall be home by six. So, you understand. And now excuse me. There is no time to lose. There never is. Good morning."

Randolph left the gloomy chambers with much the same feelings, that a patient experiences, when after long suffering on a sick bed, he is at last bid "throw physic to the dogs," and begone to the sea. He seemed to be already at work, and enjoyed the exhilarating effect. With light feet and as light a heart, he hurried back to the Bull and Mouth. Helen had finished her letter, and gave it him to read: she looked over his shoulder while he wrote a postscript, saying in hyperbolical terms, how delighted he was with Mr. Winter. A porter guided the young pair to a Hampstead coach, in which they were the third part of a half dozen, and in no long time the vehicle rumbled over the stones towards Camden Town.

A squalid part of the metropolis it was they traversed, but it was forgotten when the conveyance stopped, and the announcement "Mr. Peach's, if you please, sir," summoned Randolph and Helen to alight. Clotilda was at the parlour window, and came to meet her visitors. Mr. Winter had prepared the way for them, and Randolph had only to mention his name to gain a welcome.

"Walk in, my dear sir," said the spinster, "walk in, my dear young lady. I wish Cornelius was at home. Mr. Winter spoke of Cornelius, I suppose. The lodgings? yes, it is all the first floor. Two bed-rooms and sitting-room. Cornelius says——"

No matter what. Miss Peach had preceded her guests upstairs. Helen walked to the drawing-room window, and uttered an exclamation of surprise. Buried in that old six inside convenience, she had not observed that it had been ascending a considerable hill. The front of Mr. Peach's cottage looked on a sandy lane. But the drawing-room was at the back, and well might Helen be startled, for the window she stood at commanded a view of the rich landscape lying between the heath and Harrow. Five minutes afterwards the bargain was struck, and in five minutes more Randolph was on his way back into the city in quest of the boxes and bags, leaving Helen to become acquainted with their future hostess.

A quaint but genial pair of humourists were Cornelius and Clotilda Peach. Mr. Shandy would perhaps have attributed some of their oddity to the chance which gave them their names. A row of folio volumes in the parlour might afford some key to the brother's tastes, and would intimate that he was fond of old poems, old plays, and old divinity. Here and there a bit of paper peeping from the leaves, and written upon, betrayed some scribbling propensity on the part of the owner. Manly and kindly were all his favourite authors, and if the latter quality predominated in himself, it was only perhaps because the former had never been called into activity. Everyone who knew him loved Cornelius Peach.

And his sister loved him best. She looked up to him also, as something great. She never contradicted him, except at whist, a game in which they both rejoiced. In all other matters, when she had quoted the opinion of Cornelius, she considered the question at issue decided. A small garden was attached to the cottage, and Clotilda piqued herself on her pansies and carnations, but never grudged a flower for her brother's button-hole. Sometimes, but very rarely, her sisterly care was tried by the effect of a social party upon his uprightness, on which occasions Cornelius was apt to become sentimental about a certain Mabel whom he said he ought to have married, but whom his friends believed to be a mere phantom of his imagination. They never could learn her sirname.

Such were the worthy couple with whom the orphans of Trevethlan were now to be domesticated. When Randolph returned with the luggage, he found dinner ready for himself and Helen; and after the repast, he inquired his way to Mr. Winter's—the Elms—and left a message there, expressing his thanks, and saying how comfortably his sister and he were settled. Later in the evening a note invited them to dinner at the lawyer's the following day, which engagement they accepted with pleasure. And then, till bed-time, they were busied in arranging their goods and chattels. Mr. Peach, with thoughtful politeness, deferred an introduction till the morning.

When it came, Cornelius made his bow, and a very awkward one it was, to his new lodgers.

"Good morrow, Mr. Morton," he said, looking nowhere straight, but at Helen sideways; "good morning, Miss Morton. 'Pack clouds away, and welcome day,' I trust you have rested well. Some never can sleep in a strange bed. Yours I hope will not have that fault long."

Randolph thanked him: they had slept very well.

"Ah, Miss Morton," continued the landlord, "I would you had come earlier in the year. The fall is a sad season. Nothing in the garden but Michaelmas daisies, those miserable old bachelors of flowers; and a few chrysanthemums, the showy old maids. You will never be a chrysanthemum, Miss Morton."

The ponderous machine which called at the cottage every morning to convey Mr. Peach to the city, was now heard lumbering along the lane, and the jocund little man took his departure.

So far Randolph and Helen had scarcely found time to breathe, much less to think; but when they strolled out upon the heath in the course of the day, reflections came crowding upon their minds. The foundation of the aërial castle was fairly laid: did it promise as well, as when viewed from Merlin's Cave? Not quite perhaps. Something grated on their feelings; it might be they missed the sound of the sea; it might be the flurry through which they had passed; it might be such a trifle as the oddities of their host and hostess. The total disruption of all their old habits was more violent than they had expected. They experienced a vague uneasiness. They almost began to regret the calm of Trevethlan Castle. And when they gazed down upon the vast city, veiled by the clouds that roll continually from its myriad hearths, through which the dome of St. Paul's loomed in exaggerated dimensions, it must be confessed that their vision of the future wore a doubtful and variable hue. Their looks were downcast; gravity took the place of animation in their faces; and it was with some anxiety that they set forth on their way to the Elms.

This feeling was soon charmed away by the perfect quiet of their reception. Mr. Winter at Lincoln's Inn, and Mr. Winter at Hampstead, were very different men: there, he considered the moments as precious for work; here, they were only precious for enjoyment: there, he governed them; here, he yielded to them. A shade of impatience might be detected in his manner at chambers; nothing ruffled him at home. And Mrs. Winter, accustomed as she had always been to see only the sunny side of things, ministered admirably to the happiness of all around her, and particularly of her husband. They and their eldest daughter Emily, a blue-eyed girl with light hair, were in the drawing-room, when Randolph and Helen arrived. Before dinner was announced, the orphans had forgotten all their solicitude.

And except that they talked with rather too much preciseness, too much like a book as people say, they acquitted themselves very well in the gentle stream of conversation which their host kept tranquilly flowing. And by the time that Mrs. Winter rose to retire, they felt that they had been introduced to a new pleasure, that of agreeable society.

"So, Mr. Morton," the lawyer then said, "you wish to prepare yourself for our English forum: as honourable an arena as the Roman, although our advocates do accept of fees. Are you acquainted with the mysteries of initiation?"

Randolph referred to the old editions of Blackstone and Burn. Mr. Winter apprehended, but did not say, that there might be something to unlearn.

"Faith," said he, "the process has more to do with beef than with Blackstone; you eat your way, rather than read it. True, the sign-posts and mile-stones are not to be neglected, but you may arrive at the full dignity of wig and gown, without having turned a leaf. I don't say that is the way to turn a penny."

"It is with the last purpose that I aspire to the dignity," Randolph said, "and very much obliged to you shall I be for any advice which may further it."

"And happy I shall be to give the best I can, Mr. Morton," observed Winter. "The first step is to enter at an Inn of Court. There are four. Divers bits of doggerel describe their respective merits. Have you any predilection?"

"No, Mr. Winter," Randolph answered, "none: I am ignorant of their distinguishing peculiarities."

"Lincoln's Inn is the largest, Gray's the smallest of the societies," said Winter. "The Temples are intermediate. The Middle famous for its fine hall, the Inner for its fine garden. No well-defined professional advantages attaching to any one. It is a matter of whim. What say you?"

"One of the Temples," replied Randolph, "and I prefer the garden to the hall."

"So be it," the lawyer said. "Anything but indecision. The Inner Temple wins. Come down to town with me in the morning, and I will introduce you. And after that you must, in the first place, work; and in the second place, work; and in the third place, work. Fill your glass, Mr. Morton."

"The work should be directed, I suppose," Randolph observed, obeying the invitation.

"Certainly," said Winter. "But I'll tell you what. Let me direct you for two months or so. Take the run of my office. See a little of the actual practice of the law. And then you will go into a pleader's chambers, with a sense of the reality of your business, which increases at once both its interest and its profit."

In accepting the offer thus made, Randolph little thought how short lived its fruits were destined to be. Man proposes, Heaven disposes. There was a certain poetry in the visions of Trevethlan Castle, which veiled the real prosiness of the orphans' scheme. They knew nothing of the world. And as they walked home that evening under the stars, and thought that so they were shining upon their native towers, the doubts of the morning again beset them, and they retired to rest with foreboding hearts.

The next day Mr. Winter drove Randolph to Lincoln's Inn. "Now," said the lawyer, when they alighted in Chancery Lane, "that is the way to the Temple. Prowl about; look at the garden, and the dingy buildings around it. Ask for the treasurer's office. There say you wish to enter as a student for the bar. They'll give you a paper. Bring it to me. But take your time. Be here again at one."

Obeying these instructions, the neophyte traversed the hurrying throng of Fleet Street, and passed under the ancient arch that forms the portal of Inner Temple Lane, not without a momentary recollection of Dante's famous "All hope abandon, you who enter here." He felt immediately that he was in the toils; law stationers on each hand showed their red tape, and quills, and parchment, polite slips of the latter presenting King George's greeting to his sheriff of what county you will; dapper clerks were bustling along with bundles of paper; every door-post was crowded with a host of names, among which Randolph might recognize some he had been used to read in the newspaper. He passed under the porch of the church, recalling the days when the sword was more powerful than the pen; read the inscription recording the fire and rebuilding of the cloister; and looked with respect on the powdered wigs in the hairdresser's window. He felt benumbed by the high, dismal, worm-eaten buildings, but was relieved when the sound of falling water attracted his eye to the fountain, flinging its column of silver into the air amidst elms and sycamores. Hastening towards this green spot, he saw the hall of which Mr. Winter had spoken, and proceeded to the stairs leading to the quiet little garden, one of the pleasantest retreats in all London. Randolph gazed some time on this oasis in the legal desert, and then turned to fulfil the rest of his mission. And now he marked the many singular dials, fixed aloft against the buildings, so that one or other was always available, reminding the denizens of the value of the minutes by their dry mottos, "Time and tide tarry for no man," "Pereunt et imputantur," they perish and are laid to charge. Retracing his steps, he surveyed with pleasure the more spacious garden which had decided his choice of a society for his studentship.

The office which he sought was close at hand. On making his application he was provided with a printed form, and instructed to fill up the blanks and return it. With this he obtained admission to the garden, and sat down in one of the alcoves by the river-side to examine the document. Perplexity fell upon him as he read. Two barristers were to certify that they knew him, and believed him to be a gentleman. The expression awoke all the pride of a Trevethlan.

"Was my father, then, right?" he thought, gazing moodily on the water. "Is this a course meet for one of our name? To skulk among men in disguise? To beg certificates of honour? Believed to be a gentleman! Already my dream is fading away. Oh! my own sister, would we were back at Trevethlan! Yet shall I vex you too with my doubts?... Know me? Who knows me? Who in London knows Randolph Morton?"

Irresolute and half desponding, Randolph returned to Mr. Winter's. That gentleman soon solved the difficulty implied in the conclusion of the above reverie. "Come with me," he said; conducted the neophyte to some neighbouring chambers, presented him to Mr. Flotsam, and told his errand. "Happy to oblige a friend of yours, Winter," said the conveyancer, signing the paper; "hope Mr. Morton will prosper." The second signature was still more a matter of form, Mr. Winter merely sending the paper to Mr. Jetsam, with his compliments. "There," said he to Randolph, "now take it back to the Temple; refer to Mr. Flotsam as your acquaintance; and in a week or so you will hear of your admission."

It was as the lawyer said. But the new student received the announcement with feelings very different from those he had so long cherished in his home by the sea.

CHAPTER VI.

"Yon bosky dingle still the rustics name;
'Twas there the blushing maid confessed her flame.
Down yon green lane they oft were seen to hie,
When evening slumbered on the western sky.
That blasted yew, that mouldering walnut bare,
Each bears mementos of the fated pair."

KIRKE WHITE.

Wilderness Gate was the most picturesque, although not the principal entrance to the park of Pendarrel. The enclosing wall, formed of rough gray stones, and coloured with mosses and ferns, there swept inwards from the public road, leaving a space of turf, usually occupied by the geese of the neighbouring cottagers. The gate was in the centre of the recess, and opened on a long winding avenue of Scotch firs, the branches of which met overhead, and made the path slippery with their fallen spines. On either hand the eye might glance between their straight stems to some open ground beyond, of uneven surface, mostly covered with tall ferns, and chequered with birch-trees. A streamlet might be heard, but not seen, rippling along not far from the walk. Here and there the antlers of a stag would rise above the herbage, and a hare or rabbit might be occasionally seen to bound across an exposed plot of grass. The scene wore an air of neglect. The dead leaves were not swept from the paths; the brambles extended their long shoots at pleasure; the ruggedness of the ground was the work of nature. But the avenue wound gently up an eminence; the wood on each side became deeper, until, on arriving at the summit of a ridge, the visitor emerged suddenly from the dark firs, and gazed down upon the trim plantations and nicely-shorn lawns immediately surrounding the Hall. The portion of the park through which he had passed was called the Wilderness, and gave its name to the gate by which he entered.

Beside this gate, and close to the park-wall, was the lodge which Mrs. Pendarrel assigned as a dwelling to Maud Basset and Michael Sinson. They had previously resided at the farm-house occupied by the young man's father, the brother-in-law of the hapless Margaret. But the gloomy firs of Wilderness Lodge were more congenial to the disposition of the old woman than the cheerful garden of the Priory Farm, and the idle life of a gatekeeper suited Michael's habits better than the activity of his father's employment. The instructions also, which he received from Mrs. Pendarrel, raised vague ideas of future consequence in the young man's mind, and revived the hopes which had originally sprung from his connection with the family of Trevethlan. His new mistress discovered that he possessed some education, the abiding result of Polydore's teaching, and desired him to improve it, and to attend to his appearance, hinting at the same time rather than saying, that he might unobtrusively watch the proceedings at Trevethlan Castle, and report any changes he detected. These orders gratified his vanity, suited his meanness, and raised his expectations.

But the departure of the orphans seemed to deprive him of his occupation; nothing transpired to contradict the newspaper account of their intentions; and, indeed, these appeared so entirely natural, that a suspicion of incorrectness could hardly arise. None, at least, was likely to be suggested in the country. But only a brief space had elapsed, when a summons from Mrs. Pendarrel, requiring young Sinson to repair immediately to the metropolis, disturbed the serenity of Wilderness Lodge. His grandmother exulted in the news. Her only reading was in that fanatical literature, the study of which is apt either to find men mad, or to leave them so; and she was, besides, deeply versed in all the local superstitions of the district. Such lore had given her mind a sombre hue, and inclined her to indulge in the practice of vaticination. She had foretold a career of distinction for her grandson, and she fancied that he was now about to enter upon it. On the eve of his departure, his mother Cicely came to Wilderness Lodge to bid him farewell. She did not share in Maud's gratification.

"So," she said, sitting under the thatched verandah, "Mercy Page may suit herself now, I suppose; and Edward Owen need not fear another fall?"

"Mercy should know her own mind better," said Michael. "She might have had me long ago, if she pleased; 't is her own fault if it's too late now. But I don't think Owen'll win her, if I never try a fall with him again."

"Let her 'bide," muttered Maud; "let her 'bide. What want we with the folks of Trevethlan?"

"And what seeks my lady with you in London, Michael?" Cicely asked.

"I shall know when I get there, I dare say," he answered. "My lady's secrets are mine."

Cicely sighed.

"I thought you might let us know," she said.

"What I know not myself. Some office, my lady speaks of, I am to fit myself for."

"Ah! my son," continued his mother, "I do hope you'll not forget the country as well as Mercy Page. Life is wild in London, they say. Think of the poor squire."

"Think of my winsome Margaret," Maud exclaimed fiercely. "Think of her that the squire murdered! Wild! Na, na; he'll see the light."

Cicely was the only one of the family exempt from that hatred of the Trevethlans, which darkened the hue of the old woman's otherwise harmless enthusiasm, and burnt sullenly in her grandson. She had not long said her parting words, when Michael threw on his hat, shook himself free from the detaining grasp of old Maud, and walked briskly away in the direction of Trevethlan. About a mile from the castle, a rugged strip of waste land skirted the edge of the cliff over the beach, and supported a number of aged thorns, stunted and bent by the sea-breezes. It was to this spot that Michael turned his steps. The landscape was growing gray when he reached it, but there was yet sufficient light to discover the object he sought. A few strides placed him by the side of a young girl.

"Mercy," he said, in a low voice, "the first at a tryst! It is something new."

"The days are short," replied the girl, with affected indifference: "I should not have waited. Besides, you are going away, so one does not care."

"Is that your farewell, Mercy?" Michael asked.

"And why not?" she said, tossing her head. "You are a fine gentleman: going to London: to forget Mercy Page."

"Yes," answered Michael—his companion started at the word—"to forget the Mercy of to-night, but to remember another—the Mercy of old days; to forget her conceited and wilful, to remember her kind and winsome. You would not wish me remember the first—would you, Mercy?"

The maiden said nothing in reply; and Sinson, encouraged by her silence, drew her with gentle force to a seat on a bank of turf.

"Do you smell the wild thyme, Mercy?" he continued. "They call it a figure of love, rewarding with sweetness even what bruises it. It is so I have answered all your coldness. Mind you not the St. John's Eve, when the folks had caught you in the rope? Who fought his way to your help? And then you sat by my side on this very bank under the hawthorn; and when I asked, might I woo you?—you know what you said. And have I ever failed in my suit? Did I ever court another? When you were cross, and would not dance with me, did I seek any one else? Whose colours did I wear when I threw, one after another, all the best of Penwith? Yet, from that first evening, never could I win a civil word. And now I am called far away, Mercy will give me no hope. When I come back, she will be another's."

"No," said the maiden, and stopped short.

"Then why will she not be mine now?" asked Michael. "Why will she not go with me to London; there to be wed, and live together in happiness? Shall it not be so, dear Mercy? Alone in the great town, I shall always be thinking of Mercy—be thinking that she may be listening to Edward Owen, whom he has often thrown for her sake——"

"And shalt throw him again," interrupted a manly voice. "Shalt throw him again, or take a fall thyself."

The individual whom Michael had named stood before the astonished pair. Sinson sprang to his feet. Was it the duskiness of the evening, or passion, that made his face so dark?

"Owen," he said, in a fierce whisper, "thou wert best stand off now, or mayst get more than a fall."

"Come on!" cried his antagonist, without attempting to disguise his anger. "Come on, villain! I'm ready for you."

Fortunately perhaps for Michael, who was not in a mood to fight or wrestle fairly, Mercy interposed.

"Hoity-toity!" she cried; "pray, Master Edward, where did you learn to give such names to your betters? And where did you learn to follow honest people's steps, and watch them? And think you, my—do you hear?—my Michael is to fight with such as you? Go home, and learn manners."

"Oh, Mercy!" cried Owen, "you know not what you say. You know not what he means. But my part is done. Remember, Edward Owen's is not the only heart you'll break. And so, good-night."

He turned and walked steadily away. Michael endeavoured to resume the thread of his previous discourse. But his listener's mood was entirely changed.

"Saucy fellow!" she cried, laughing and looking after Owen; "he's a rare one to come and rate me. But do you know, Mr. Michael, I believe he's a better man than you. There, that will do. To London to be married! No, Mr. Michael, not quite so far, if you please. Oh, yes, of course. D'ye think I like fighting? There. Good-night, Mr. Michael. No. If you follow me, I shall call him back."

She disengaged herself from her suitor, and tripped lightly through the gloom in the footsteps of Owen.

Michael watched her retreating form with a scowl darker even than that with which he rose to meet the intruder upon his courtship. "Shalt rue the day"—

he muttered, "shalt rue the day that saw thee cross my wooing. A better man than me, did she say? Look to thyself, Master Edward Owen."

With a heaving breast and an irregular gait, Sinson paced to and fro for some time along the edge of the cliff, and then turned moodily to Wilderness Lodge. The next day he departed on his way to London.

CHAPTER VII.

"Il y a dans un mariage malheureux une force qui dépasse toutes les autres peines de ce monde."

MADAME DE STAËL.

The summons which called Michael Sinson from the far-west to the metropolis, was the result of impulse rather than of settled design on the part of his patroness. Quick in reading the characters of all who crossed her path, in her first brief colloquy with the rustic, Mrs. Pendarrel detected his animosity towards Trevethlan; and in his sly but fierce countenance, in his well-built but cringing form, she saw the traits of one who would not be scrupulous in his mode of attacking an enemy. From the very first, she suspected that the announced continental tour of the orphans was a ruse, and the notion gained strength whenever it recurred to her mind. But if they were still in England, they were probably abiding in London. She caught at the idea, and thought suddenly it would be well to have some one at hand who knew them personally.

Suspiciousness is natural to tyranny: spies are the agents of despots. Love of rule, said by the fairy to be the universal passion of the sex, was undoubtedly dominant in Mrs. Pendarrel. But it is a desire which, at least in youth, will find one powerful rival. And so she proved. The haughty beauty kept her affection down with a strong hand, but it stung her nevertheless. The wound rankled ever in her heart; and many a time and oft she cast a rapid glance upon her life, and in momentary weakness compared what was indeed a dark reality, with a visionary possibility whose very glory made her sad.

But though such reflections might sadden, they were far from softening her. They always terminated in the conviction that she had been ill used. As years sped by, and each showed her more plainly the vacancy of her existence, this feeling deepened into a quenchless thirst for revenge. Was she to be the only victim? Man had a hundred means of quelling or forgetting a hapless passion. Should he who had so lightly forsaken her—should he triumph while her heart was broken?

He threw the game into her hands, and died. Towards his children she entertained at the moment no very definite feeling. She had scarcely thought of them. But she had long cherished the idea of becoming mistress of Trevethlan Castle, and at last she deemed the hour was arrived. Met according to her expectations, she would probably have been kind to the orphans. Spurned, as she felt it, from their door, hatred burnt again fiercely in her breast. And it was quickened by a strange jealousy she conceived against their mother, whom she had only despised before, but now bitterly envied as the wife of her lover.

Could domestic happiness be expected with such a parent? Alas, for the answer which would come from Mrs. Pendarrel's children! The angry passions which raged in her breast gave an unmotherly hardness to her love of rule. And why were they daughters? *He* had a son. *She*, the wretched peasant, was the mother of a son. Thus did the effects of Esther's blighted affection fall even upon her offspring. But Gertrude rebelled from early childhood against the capricious rigour with which she was treated. She succumbed at last, however, and that in the most important event of her life. In obeying the maternal command to marry Mr. Winston, she thought she stooped to conquer. Gertrude Winston would be her own mistress. And so she was; but at what a price! Ay, what an account must they render, who degrade marriage into a convenience! who banish the household deities, so dear even to ancient paganism, from their place beside the hearth, and fill it with furies and fiends! who know not the meaning of our sweet English name of home! Five years had not reconciled Gertrude to a union in which her heart had no share. Her husband seemed to her cold, prudent, and dull. She was enthusiastic, generous, and clever. He was easy and good-natured, and his very submissiveness fretted her. He was, or pretended to be, fond of metaphysics, and was always engaged upon some terribly ponderous tome, while she participated in the popular fury for Byron and Scott. He liked a level road, and a good inn: she delighted in romantic scenery, and was half careless about the accommodation. They continually pulled against each other; but the husband was insensible to the chain which galled the wife to the quick. Yet Mr. Winston possessed qualities, which only required to be known to be beloved, and if Gertrude was ignorant of them, it was in no small degree her own fault. And she had not, like Mrs. Pendarrel, to contend with the memory of a previous attachment.

But, however bitter might be the feelings with which she contemplated her own position, there was one dear affection which she cherished with the utmost fondness. Nothing could exceed her solicitude to preserve her sister from the snares into which she had fallen herself. She kept a watchful eye upon all the society especially favoured by her mother, and observed Mildred's feelings with the warmest interest. And she was met in the same spirit. Sisterly love was the one humanizing tie in that broken family.

Each sister possessed great personal attractions; but though their features were strikingly alike, the character written on their faces was by no means the same. Gertrude's showed haughty indifference, Mildred's wishful thoughtfulness. The elder's smile was generally sarcastic, the younger's sympathetic. Knowledge of her situation, and consciousness that others knew it, flashed in defiance from the dark eyes of Mrs. Winston, and lent a *hardiesse* to her tongue, which occasionally seemed unfeminine. Trust and hope beamed from beneath the long lashes of Miss Pendarrel, and her speech was commonly soft and gentle; but in society she was lively and witty, and there was a spirit lurking in her heart, which might one day confound even her mother.

Coming one day about this time to May Fair, Gertrude found a gentleman of her acquaintance sitting with Mrs. Pendarrel and Mildred.

"Dear mamma," Mrs. Winston said, as she entered, "I am come to claim Mildred for an hour's drive.—Delighted to see you, Mr. Melcomb. You can settle a little dispute for me. 'Tis about the colour of the Valdespini's eyes."

"I would prefer to leave it to Mr. Winston," answered Melcomb. "He has some strange theory about colours, that they are in the eyes of the seer and not in the seen. It is dangerous to speak after such an authority. Your best referee is at home, Mrs. Winston."

"Not so," said the lady, "for he is one of the disputants. One said blue, another grey. None agreed. Some one suggested a reference to you, and it was voted unanimously. 'He knows the colour of all the eyes at the opera,' they said."

"No one can mistake that of Mrs. Winston's," Melcomb said, rising and bowing. "My dear Mrs. Pendarrel, suffer me to take my leave."

"Now, Mildred dear, away and make ready," said Gertrude, smiling, and her sister immediately complied with the wish.

"Mrs. Winston!" exclaimed the mother.

"Yes, dear mamma," Gertrude answered.

"Am I the mistress of my own house?"

"I presume so, dear mamma."

"Then note me. My visitors shall not be affronted here by you."

"Surely, mamma, Mr. Melcomb would thank me for a compliment. Every one knows he is proud of his reputation."

"Every one knows your sarcasm," said Mrs. Pendarrel, "and I, at least, perfectly understand your meaning. Once for all, Mrs. Winston, I will suffer no interference with my intentions for Mildred. Why, I almost think you would not have her settled at all. Very sisterly indeed, Gertrude. Yet in your situation——"

"Mother," exclaimed Mrs. Winston, "not another word. But listen. Rather than see Mildred settled even as I am, without offence, as without affection,

- 45 -

I know not to what I would not doom her! Rather than see her wedded to one like Melcomb, would she might die in my sight! You know me, mother. She is here."

"There's no danger, Gertrude," said Mrs. Pendarrel, as Mildred entered; "au revoir."

The sisters then descended the stairs. As they passed through the hall, they might have observed the presence of a young man, not in livery, plainly dressed, having an appearance of *mauvaise honte* not often imputable to the denizens of London. They might have noticed that after the first glimpse he caught of Mildred, his gaze was rivetted upon her face, and the colour deepened in his cheeks as she approached and swept by him, almost brushing him with the trimming of her mantle. But in fact, they saw nothing of the kind, passing along in polite indifference to Mrs. Winston's carriage.

"And so, Mildred," that lady said, as they drove away, "another admirer! You are growing quite a coquette."

"Not exactly," answered the younger sister. "But I like to amuse myself with the vanity of men. After all, I wish I were married."

Mrs. Winston sighed. "At another time, Mildred dear," she said, "I might rally you for the avowal. But beware. Marriage is a sad lottery."

"You are happy, Gertrude," said Mildred with some surprise.

Mrs. Winston looked out of her window.

"Melcomb will never make a woman happy," she said, after a pause.

"He will certainly never make me happy," exclaimed Mildred, half laughing. "But really, Gertrude, how silly I am! What does Mr. Melcomb care about me!"

"Very little, I dare say, not to flatter you, dear. Very little about Mildred: a good deal about Mildred's money. And perhaps mamma would not care to add Tolpeden to Pendarrel. You know they join. There's something for your cogitation."

For a while the sisters were silent. Then the younger spoke.

"Dearest Gertrude," she said, "believe me I will never marry without— believe me, I have not yet seen anyone whom I would marry. When I spoke just now, I hardly knew what I meant."

Poor Gertrude knew her sister's meaning perfectly well. She recollected the weight of the chain from which she had recklessly made her escape, without calculating the cost.

"Mildred," said she, "let me ever be your confidante as now."

And so in a less serious mood, the sisters pursued their way round the November dreariness of Hyde Park, at the season when:—

"Remote, unfriended, solitary, slow, Scarce one lone horseman paces Rotten Row."

The stranger they had passed in Mrs. Pendarrel's vestibule was Michael Sinson, newly arrived in London, and come with proper diligence to pay his respects to his patroness. The young countryman was completely overwhelmed by the vision of the two fine ladies who swept by him. But his wonder was not indiscriminating, and it was Mildred who fixed his gaze. He had seen her at Pendarrel, but not with the same impression. In kind and familiar intercourse with the tenantry, she was a very different person. Here she seemed almost a creature of another sphere. With her mien, so quiet and yet so proud; her step, scarcely touching the ground, yet appearing to spurn it; her repose, exhibiting a security which it was impossible to disturb. Michael followed her with his eyes until she had entered the carriage, and continued looking vacantly in the same direction, even after the hall-door was closed. A tap on the shoulder roused him from his abstraction, and he followed a servant into the presence of Mrs. Pendarrel.

The interview was of no great duration. Sinson's patroness was pleased to notice with praise that he was improved in appearance and address; and asked him a few questions respecting the country, which he answered to her satisfaction. She made no allusion to the peculiar services she expected from him, but referred him to her husband at his office for information respecting his promised employment. It was necessary to know a little more of his temper and disposition before making him her confidential agent.

The new Cymon, as in one sense the young rustic might be called, quitted the house in May Fair, filled with vague admiration and ambition. In the fascinations surrounding Miss Pendarrel, he recognised a power superior to anything within his experience; and he framed fantastic expectations from the career he supposed opening before him. But the lover of Iphigenia had concealed a noble heart under a rugged exterior, and his passion developed its high qualities. Michael Sinson was a very different character from Boccaccio's hero.

And was Mercy Page already forgotten?—Happy, perchance, for the too faithful maiden, if so it were.

CHAPTER VIII.

"Nam veluti pueri trepidant, atque omnia cœcis
  In tenebris metuunt, sic nos in luce timemus
Interdum, nihilo quæ sunt metuenda magis, quam
  Quæ pueri in tenebris pavitant, finguntque futura."

LUCRET.

  As children tremble, and in darkness quake
  At all things near, so we too sometimes shake
  At daylight fancies, vain as those which scare
Children in darkness with foreboding fear.

They were not halcyon days in England that succeeded the termination of the long struggle for liberty and existence, which, during more than twenty years, had taxed to the uttermost all the resources of the country; and which, as a whole, must always be regarded by Britons with pride and exultation. We had given peace to the world; but we were unable to preserve tranquillity at home. War is, at the best, a bad education, if sometimes a necessary one, for a young people; and a mature nation will find that its costs are not only money and men. It is a lottery on the grandest scale, both of fortune and life, inducing waste of the one, and recklessness of the other; removing, therefore, in a great measure, the vulgar motives of action, and importing a general laxity of principle. In various ways a long war produces an intestinal feverishness, aggravating any incidental disorder, and favourable to the designs of incendiaries.

The peace was followed by a general fall in wages. It was a result beyond the control of legislation; and it would probably have been unfelt, if prices also had fallen, as naturally they should have done. But the legislature was able in part to prevent this decline, and exercised its power in favour of agricultural produce. Flaming homesteads and shattered machinery soon proclaimed the discontent of the labouring population.

Political agitators sought to turn this discontent into disaffection. Parliamentary reform was demanded with a considerable show of violence. There was much fierce speaking; numbers of clubs started into existence; individuals disfigured themselves with strange costumes; mobs collected in great multitudes. Presently budding Lafayettes discussed the most convenient length for pikes, and would-be Buonapartes mustered their platoons by moonlight.

There was a good deal that was wicked, and not a little that was grotesque, in these proceedings. One party persisted in seeing only the white side of the shield, and declared they were merely ridiculous; another had eyes only for the black, and exaggerated their danger. Nothing is so fatal to the cause of civil liberty as the abuse of the privileges which it confers. The nation consents to wear chains, to control a rebellious member. Having the gout in its great toe, the body politic restricts its indulgences. It was so at the period of which we are treating. The real amount of danger is a question which the candour of posterity will admit could hardly be discussed with tranquillity at the time. Certain it is, that alarm was very great and very general, and under its pressure the nation resigned for a season some of its dearest birth-rights. Personal liberty was endangered by the suspension of the Habeas Corpus Act; the press was shackled; the right of meeting was limited. Arrests were made far and wide. A north-country squire, trotting quietly along upon his hack to meet the hounds, was swept off to jail, instead of sweeping after the fox, suspected of a design to raise the shepherds. It was a mistake, and it is probable that such were not rare. The practice of receiving information from spies, and still more the air of mystery assumed by those in authority, multiplied the apprehensions which might justly be excited by any tumultuous proceedings.

Cornelius Peach was one of those who were willing to believe the alarm to be in the main unfounded, and he used good-humouredly to quiz his sister for the timidity with which she adopted every rumour of the day. The worthy clerk was clearly in some matters a follower of the philosopher of Abdera. He very much preferred laughter to tears; regarded public affairs with a lofty disdain, so long as his roast, boiled, or hashed was ready at the right time; lived in a Utopia of his own, and was more likely to die of seeing an ass eating figs than of any ordinary calamity. He could not understand why an individual should fret himself concerning parliamentary corruption, tyranny of government, abuse of patronage, or any other stalking-horse of sedition. No one had attempted to bribe him; he felt indifferently free; he was a candidate for no place; he had no vote for anything, and rejoiced that he had not. His even cheerfulness was wont to make his friends declare, that their Peach was all sunny side; there were no signs of shade about him.

His lodger was of a less contented mood: the symptoms of effervescence had assumed a somewhat menacing aspect around his home. For some time much disquiet had prevailed among the miners of Somersetshire, and the same was now rapidly spreading among their Cornish brethren, from Redruth to St. Ives. Minor outrages were of no uncommon occurrence. The dread which Miss Peach seemed to entertain of seeing a modern Jack Straw encamped on Hampstead Heath, was felt on better grounds in the far-west, and caused trepidation among the tea-sipping gossips of Kerrier and Penwith. So the orphans learnt from the letters of Polydore Riches. And they were made rather anxious by perceiving, that the good chaplain seemed in writing, to disguise the real amount of his apprehensions. Often in reading his missives, did Randolph and Helen turn their thoughts fondly towards Trevethlan, and wish they had never left the towers by the sea.

And in the brother such yearnings were quickened by an ever-increasing discontent with his position. This feeling had soon driven him from Winter's chambers, and he was now reading with Mr. Travers, an eminent special pleader. But dissatisfaction was again creeping over him. It was true he did not neglect his studies, and he had duly eaten his dinners to keep Michaelmas Term. Surely there is no fear that any of our old institutions to which a dinner is attached will wholly die. There is a strength in the British appetite, against which utilitarianism may struggle in vain, till hunger and thirst are no more. So at the Inns of Court. The exercises, and moots, and even the revels have vanished, but the dinners remain. Attendance on the former has been commuted into fines to maintain the latter. And long may they endure, those social meetings, where many a lasting friendship is formed, and the bonds of brotherhood cemented, which in England unite an order, declared by D'Aguesseau, *aussi ancien que la magistrature, aussi noble que la vertu, aussi nécessaire que la justice.*

As a novice, Randolph was partly interested and partly disconcerted on his introduction to these assemblies. He felt a reverence for the old hall, standing on the site of that of the knights whose dust reposed in the neighbouring church. He looked with respect on the coats of arms of the successive treasurers, emblazoned on the oak panelling of the walls, and subscribed with many a name of high distinction. On the dais, beneath the portraits of Littleton and Coke, sat some of the leading advocates of the day, partaking a more luxurious repast than that allotted to the occupants of the floor below. And on the opposite side to the young student were the juniors of the bar, men who had risen, were rising, had not begun to rise, and never would rise.

It was all curious and new. The very gown in which Randolph dined, rustled on his shoulders with a forensic feeling. The repast was apportioned to messes of four, all of which had precisely the same fare. The attendants were called *paniers*; because—an enemy has suggested—supported by donkeys. The platters were of Peter Piper's metal, and the cups were earthenware. As at the table of Prior's pococurante couple—

"Their ale was strong, their wine was port, Their meal was large, their grace was short."

Trifles all these: forgotten perhaps by the fortunate lawyer, whose clerk groans under the weight of his brief-bag; ridiculed by the disappointed man, whose early clients have long disappeared; but interesting and entertaining to the neophyte, whose ambition foresees the career of the first, whose self-reliance is too strong to fear the fate of the second.

These last were the feelings which had inspired Randolph in the solitude of Trevethlan Castle, and conjured up those airy visions which seemed so fair in the sight of himself and his sister. The very first encounter with the world had dimmed the prospect for a moment, and the brother's subsequent intercourse with it confirmed rather than diminished his disappointment. It was not that he was disheartened by perceiving how very inadequate an idea he had formed of the labour necessary to attain his object. The long rows of law-calf on Mr. Travers's shelves had no terrors for him. Nor was it that he felt as yet any decided uneasiness at living under a feigned name. He had never for an instant imagined it was wrong, and it had his father's sanction. Yet this circumstance might be a chief source of his discontent. He had not known the levelling tendency of a public school, nor the freedom of college. From those early lessons in the picture-gallery at Trevethlan, he had silently grown up in the consciousness that he should be the head of an ancient race, and perhaps, in building his castle in the air, he regarded himself as an architect in the midst of masons. He never thought of himself as Morton, humble and unknown, but as the representative of a high family, recognized and honoured.

So Mr. Griffith was right, and Polydore Riches wrong. But the worthy chaplain was in no fault. No education could have prevailed against the circumstances of the case. A youth spent in isolation and reverie, is almost certain to lead to a manhood of irresolution. The habit of thinking becomes a curse, when it is developed too early. Such precociousness is apt to result in a purely negative character. This was the misfortune of Randolph. And although he carefully pursued his studies, and concealed his disquietude from Helen, he often sighed for the peace of his home, and sometimes even thought of abandoning his scheme, and returning thither.

The same feelings made him distant and reserved in his intercourse with the men in Hall and at Mr. Travers's chambers. He had no sympathy with their buoyancy, and he disliked their familiarity. There was, however, one of the latter, with whom he grew gradually intimate, having been introduced to him by Mr. Winter. Seymour Rereworth was a man of calm but decided opinions, of quiet and diligent habits, of polished manners, and of great attainments. He possessed also the advantages which Randolph missed so much, having been educated at Eton, and having obtained high honours at college. Looking to his profession for distinction more than actual maintenance, he earnestly and steadily pursued his aim, never revolting from the weary drudgery, never disheartened by the thorny intricacies, through which the lawyer is doomed to plod in his way to eminence. Very particular in his choice of friends, he was interested by the mixture of enthusiasm and embarrassment which he detected in Randolph, and sought his friendship. Where Rereworth sought, he won. And he was of great service to his companion, supplying his want of knowledge of the world with his own, which was of the best kind; not consisting in a familiarity with knavery and vice, but able to foil the one and repel the other; and excelling in all those qualities which are comprised in the word, tact. He had a large acquaintance in society; was himself very well connected; was always a welcome guest, and, when he chose to throw away an evening, had always an invitation available.

Him did Randolph once or twice, during the winter, persuade to come and spend an evening at Hampstead. And it must be confessed that Seymour paid his second visit at least as willingly as his first. If he liked the brother, he no less admired the sister. He mused sometimes on the circumstances of so singular, he might say so romantic, a pair. Helen's dark and gentle eyes, and soft and pleasant tones, haunted him occasionally in his studies, and kept his pen suspended in the midst of many a tedious draught. But Rereworth was not a man to fall in love in a hurry.

For Helen, she was always glad to see him. In spite of all her brother's precautions, she sometimes detected the gloom and discontent which hung upon his brow, and she saw that Rereworth's society always charmed them away. Her own life was so tranquil and uniform that she had soon ceased to regret the quiet of Trevethlan, and she roamed about the vicinity of Hampstead, seeking a spot she might liken to Merlin's Cave, and only occasionally disturbed by the letters of Polydore Riches.

***

CHAPTER IX.

Romeo.—What lady's that, which doth enrich the hand
Of yonder Knight?

Servant.—   I know not, sir.

Romeo.—O, she doth teach the torches to burn bright!
Her beauty hangs upon the cheek of night,
Like a rich jewel in an Ethiop's ear:
Beauty too rich for use, for earth too dear!

SHAKSPEARE.

So the winter passed on. Christmas might remind the orphans of a custom which prevailed in the Cornwall of old times, and which may possibly still survive in some localities, when the family of each homestead bore a bowl of cider in jocund procession to their orchard, and, selecting the most respectable apple-tree, splashed his trunk with the bright liquor, and wished him good luck in the coming season. "Would," exclaimed Cornelius Peach, with great unction, when Helen told him the story, "would that I had been born in some strange, half-barbarous land! These great towns kill all good customs. Even what little carol-singing there is, is a mere trade."

Christmas passed, and the new year was destined to introduce Helen to another order of singing. Thirty years ago the London season began earlier than at present. January was not over, when a note from Mrs. Winter invited the brother and sister to accompany her to the opera. A vague excitement rose in Helen's breast, and sparkled in her eyes, as she gave the note to Randolph. She felt that she should like to go, but a certain shyness made her timid. She watched her brother's face while he glanced over the invitation, and saw with some regret that he did not partake her anticipations. But he said that it was very kind of Mrs. Winter, and that of course they would go.

On the appointed evening the lawyer's carriage called for the orphans, and they joined him and his wife. It was a gloomy ride. The night was foggy and dark. The mist condensed on the windows, and permitted nothing to be seen but the general glare of the lamps. This sort of isolation, and the continuous rumble of the carriage, suited Randolph's mood. He was haunted by forebodings of evil. He was angry with himself for accepting the invitation. He felt an indefinite fear of the crowd with which he was about to mingle. It was not as Morton that he ought to appear in public. Yet should his selfish pride debar Helen of the offered amusement? He leant back in his corner of the carriage, abstracted and silent.

His sister on the other hand was gay and excited. She kept up a lively conversation with Mr. and Mrs. Winter, and peered through the window at what was to her an unknown world. So it was until the carriage turned a corner, and entered a broader and better-lighted thoroughfare than those it had traversed previously. Its speed abated: it even stopped—were they there? No, it moves again: papers are pressed against the glasses: another pause, and another advance: and now Mr. Winter has lowered his window, the door is opened, the steps let down, and before Helen has time to think, she finds herself leaning upon his arm, and ascending a spacious staircase. She looks round, and sees her brother and Mrs. Winter close behind.

A few minutes more, and she stood in the front of a box, and gazed on a vast area, dimly lighted by a circle of small lustres immediately beneath her, and an immense chandelier far above. They were very early; but few boxes were occupied, the foot-lights were not raised, and the orchestra was nearly empty. The dark green of the great curtain seemed almost black in the gloom. Helen asked Mrs. Winter if it were not very dark.

"Ah! wait a moment," said that lady.

And in fact, even as she spoke, a row of bright lamps rose in front of the curtain, and a flood of splendour from the central chandelier irradiated the whole house, displaying the occupants of the boxes, as portraits set in frames of rich crimson. A rustle of conversation murmured from the pit, but was soon lost in the confused sounds which came from the orchestra, now rapidly filling. With a wild kind of surprise Helen listened to those discordant tones, and noted how by degrees they melted into harmony with the leader's long-drawn note. At length there was silence; a gentleman with a small wand took his place at a desk in front of the musicians, talking and laughing with those near him; a little bell rang behind the curtain; and after three taps of the wand, the orchestra whirled away into the overture to an opera then new to a London audience, never to become antiquated.

The foot-lights sank, and the great green curtain rose. The stage was nearly dark. A droll-looking personage came stealthily forward, bowing in acknowledgment of the applause, or of the laughter, which greeted his appearance. Helen laughed, without knowing why. She had a book, but she was too much absorbed to consult it, and kept her eyes fixed on the stage. The droll-looking man sang a whimsical complaint, and retreated from approaching footsteps. There was a struggle between a gentleman and a lady, interrupted by an old man in a night-cap. The old man was killed. There was passionate lamentation over his body. There were scenes, of which Helen scarcely knew whether they were comic or serious. Then came a rural festival which raised her spirits; the gentleman she had seen at first, now courted one of the country girls; hand in hand they quitted the stage, amidst a hurricane of applause. But Helen was unconscious of the enthusiasm around her, so strongly was she impressed by the music. She had heard Ambrogetti and Fodor sing *La ci darem.*

The duet was repeated with nearly the same effect. And for the novices, for Randolph as well as Helen, this was the great stage sensation of the night. Other portions of the opera, Zerlina's touching remonstrance with her jealous lover, the prayer, the whirlwind of passion in which the first act terminates, the semi-grotesque marvels of the second with their wonderful music, all excited more or less emotion; but none so fresh and absorbing as that induced by the immortal duet between the peasant-girl and the profligate.

And a particular circumstance distracted Randolph's attention during the second act. In the interval which followed the first, Mrs. Winter called her young friends' notice to the house, then very well filled, instructed them in its technicalities, and pointed out a few notable personages among the audience, whom she happened to know by sight. While in this manner she was directing Randolph's eye along the tier of boxes level with her own, his regard fell upon a young lady of so remarkable an aspect, that after mechanically following Mrs. Winter's instruction, he turned hastily to look once more at his fair neighbour. Never in his life, he thought, had he seen so attractive an object. She was evidently engaged in an animated conversation with some one in the back of the box whom he could not see. Playfulness sparkled in her otherwise soft eyes, archness curved her brows, and Randolph almost imagined he could hear the silvery laugh which parted her lips. He tried to obtain a glimpse of the happy person to whom she was talking, but the attempt was vain. He could only discover that with her there was an elderly lady, whose back was turned towards him. It was not to her that the sallies of the young one were addressed. Randolph began to construct a romance, still gazing on the interesting box. Suddenly he caught his charmer's eye. It was but for a moment; he could not see that the expression of her face varied in the most trifling particular; yet he felt that he blushed like fire, and he perceived that the elder lady leant forward, and looked towards him. What, thought he, lowering his eyes for an instant, and pursuing his romance, is she so quick in detecting a glance? It must be the mother. The thought passed, and he looked up. He encountered the supposed mother's gaze fixed full upon his face. Had he not seen those features before? Ideas raced through his mind with a dream-like rapidity. Some theorists say that the visions of a night are contained in the moment of falling asleep. Surely equally swift was the flight of that lady's thoughts; or why, after a look of a single second, did her countenance assume that expression of scorn or defiance? An expression quite apart from any which might have rebuked the intrusive stare of a stranger; which even attracted the notice of her companion, who glanced again at Randolph, and then at his sister.

From that time, Randolph's attention was almost entirely engrossed by his fascinating neighbour. He missed the statue's nod, and lost his share of the laugh at Naldi's comic terror. His sister observed the cause of his abstraction, and looked in the same direction, at a moment when the elder lady happened to turn towards her.

"Surely," Helen exclaimed, "I have seen that face before! Yet how can it be?"

Randolph knew right well, but he was silent.

"Do you know those ladies, Mrs. Winter?" Helen asked.

"No, Miss Morton. It is really a beautiful girl."

"Beautiful!" Randolph thought; "beautiful! Ay, she is more than beautiful."

And the presentiment he had felt before came gloomily back upon his heart.

But the fair stranger was not the only damsel who attracted admiration in the opera-house that night.

"Who is that, Melcomb?" asked a portly, good-humoured personage, leaning on the rail of the orchestra, and looking towards Mrs. Winter's box. "A new face, is it not?"

"The girl with the bird of paradise in her hair?" answered Melcomb. "Fie! Winesour. Have you forgotten Cressy?—Though, to be sure, the gentle Cressida may have a new face to-night, or any night."

"Pooh! you know who I mean," Winesour persisted; "in the tier below."

"The pallid thing in black?" said Melcomb. "It's in a state of willowhood. You see through a glass of Chambertin."

"May I never drink another," cried Winesour, with a quaint twinkle of his small grey eye, "if she ever saw an opera before. Think you I have no eyes? *Vorrei e non vorrei.* She followed Fodor's notes with her lips apart, and tears in her eyes. She cried, Melcomb."

"Winesour turned enthusiastic for a pale-cheeked girl!" said Melcomb. "What next? But I love not rhapsody, so—adieu!"

But while he chose to speak of Helen's appearance in these disparaging terms, Melcomb had really observed her with admiration, and determined to ascertain who she might be. He was one of those handsome, careless, profligate fellows, who are too well regarded by the men, and too easily pardoned by the women. One murder, it has been rather absurdly said, makes a villain; ten thousand, a hero. But it may with some truth be remarked, that the number of hearts a Melcomb breaks rather adds to his fame than diminishes his reputation. He rises upon ruin.

Melcomb, however, was at last positively thinking of marriage, and had become the slave professed of Mildred Pendarrel. But he sped not in his wooing as he conceived he had a right to expect. Now, it is an annoying thing for one accustomed to carry the citadel by storm, to be obliged to sit down and proceed according to the slow routine of a siege; and still more disagreeable to be unable to make any impression on the enemy's works. This was Melcomb's present position. He was favoured by the mother, he was foiled by the daughter. It was a case quite out of his experience. Mildred rode with him, danced with him, flirted with him; but she never let him utter more than one serious word. The instant he assumed an air of gravity, she prevented his speech with a jest. His courtship was a perpetual laugh. It grew quite fatiguing. Love was pleasant enough, except to make. Melcomb sometimes thought of retiring from the field. He was not stimulated by difficulty, and he was afraid of rejection. Melcomb refused! What a disgrace! Yet he felt morally certain that this would be his fate, if he now ventured to drive Mildred to Yes or No. At the same time, he was unwilling to withdraw. The match would be decidedly advantageous to him, and the lady correctly ornamental. So he bore with her frolic humour as best he might. When accosted by Winesour in the pit, he had sought refuge there from Mildred's sallies; and had been struck by the strange beauty, whose earnest interest in the music seemed, indeed, to distinguish a novice, and excited a languid curiosity in the used-up coxcomb. He now returned to Mrs. Pendarrel's box, to obtain a nearer view of the fair unknown, and not without some notion of provoking Mildred's jealousy. But her mother anticipated him.

"Can you tell me," she asked, "who those ladies are, Mr. Melcomb? You know everybody."

"My knowledge is at fault," he answered. "Shall I inquire?"

"I should like to know," Mrs. Pendarrel continued; "but they are going, and so shall I."

Mrs. Winter's party, unconscious of the interest they excited, were waiting, clustered together, for the announcement of their carriage, when Mrs. Pendarrel's was declared to stop the way. At the sound of the name, Randolph and Helen involuntarily turned, and found themselves face to face with the lady who had before attracted their observation. She swept haughtily past them, without seeming to be aware of their surprise, and was followed by Mildred, leaning on the arm of Melcomb.

"It was the miniature," Helen whispered to her brother, who had become suddenly pale.

In a few moments Melcomb returned to the crush room, and observed the strangers with a well-bred stare. Randolph frowned, and the coxcomb smiled. Mrs. Winter's carriage was called. Melcomb noted the name, and learnt the destination. For the present it was enough. The beau had become too idle and indifferent to be very mischievous. He accepted a sensation if it fell in his path, but he would not go out of his way to seek one. "Hampstead's a great distance," he muttered, and drove to the Argyll Rooms.

CHAPTER X.

"He that has light within his own clear breast,
May sit in the centre, and enjoy bright day;
But he that hides a dark soul and foul thoughts,
Benighted walks under the mid-day sun:
Himself is his own dungeon."

MILTON.

Extremely startled was Mrs. Pendarrel by the appearance of the orphans of Trevethlan at the opera. Domestic affairs had temporarily diverted her suspicions respecting them, and her intentions were in a manner dormant. Great, therefore, was her surprise, when following a glance of Mildred's in which she detected some slight emotion, her own eye fell upon a face, like, yes the very image of Henry Trevethlan: the very image of what he was that fatal day, when her hasty and haughty speech drove him from her presence, for once and for ever. With a sort of fascination she gazed upon the stranger, and saw that he returned the regard with a curiosity or wonder, that changed while she looked into hatred and defiance. "Can it be possible?" she asked herself. Several times during the remainder of the performance, she turned towards Mrs. Winter's box, and never failed to catch Randolph's eye. And finally, in leaving the house, she noticed the manner in which both he and Helen started at the announcement of her name, and again met that proud resentment which she remembered so well in the lover of her girlhood.

"Winter!" she mused when she lay down for rest, "Winter! Ay, that is the name of their lawyer. I ought to know it well. And what do they here? Why this apparent privacy? Why seek this veil for their poverty? I must discover. They must be unmasked. Who knows but they are involved? What plan are they devising to save those mouldering towers?"

A long train of reflections passed through Esther's mind as she lay awake that night. In the morning she summoned Michael Sinson to her presence. The young man was already considerably improved in appearance, had lost his rusticity, and acquired a manner "free and easy," with a very excellent opinion of himself. The change might be partly due to certain vague aspirations which pleased his vanity, and at the same time sharpened his natural foresight and cunning. He was abject in deference towards his patroness.

"Sinson," said she, when he came before her, "you know Mr. Trevethlan well?"

"Certainly, ma'am; from his very cradle."

"They say, he is abroad."

He noted the words—they say. "Yes, ma'am."

"There is a Mr. Winter, a lawyer, living at Hampstead," Mrs. Pendarrel continued. "He has some friend remarkably like what I should expect ... young Trevethlan to be. I desire to find out who this person is, and what are his pursuits. Be so good as to inquire, if you can. Good morning, Sinson."

But the peasant lingered.

"Did you ever hear, ma'am," he said, brushing his hat, and casting down his eyes, "that the late Mr. Trevethlan's marriage was not regular?"

Mrs. Pendarrel lost no word of the slow-spoken insinuation. Every nerve of her body quivered, but she was silent.

"It was no blame to my unfortunate relation, ma'am," Sinson proceeded; "but the report was very common, I have heard, at Trevethlan, soon after the time."

"Pshaw! sir," Esther said, having now mastered her emotion; "common fame is a common liar. Good-day to you."

And Michael departed, well aware that his patroness suspected this friend of Mr. Winter to be no other than the heir of Trevethlan, and believing also that he had sent a shaft home to her heart, which might further the projects lurking dimly in his own. The more he advanced in her confidence the greater became his own assurance, and he now quitted the house in May Fair, with a certain exultation gleaming in his dark sinister eyes.

He had already supposed that he might find a subordinate instrument of use to him, and had even selected his man. He mingled now and then in the promiscuous assembly of vice and folly which met at the Argyll Rooms. There he had occasionally thrown away a guinea—he was liberally supplied with money—at hazard and had played at the same table with Melcomb. There also he met a man, in the smallness of whose stakes and the desperation of his play, Sinson read ruin. He paid the gambler assiduous court.

Lewis Everope had inherited a moderate patrimony, and lived as if it were inexhaustible. He had been to a university, only to squander his money, and to obtain no distinction. Confident in his abilities, he never gave them fair play. He seemed to think that intuition could supply the place of information. He rarely finished a book—did he not know what the author was about to say? Thus his knowledge was of little value, because it was never complete. Every hour a new Cynthia attracted his attention. He did almost everything by halfs, and therefore few things well. Desultory men are not often men of principle, and he was not one of the exceptions. He was fond of society, and too careless to avoid its temptations. Very soon he learned the difficulty of saying "No."

His career was much the same, when he quitted the university with a very ignoble degree, and entered an inn of court and a pleader's chambers, in the idea of being admitted to the forum. He became immersed in gay company; enjoyed, like Alfieri when an ensign in the Asti militia, the greatest possible liberty of doing nothing, which was precisely the one thing he was determined to do; in spite of the remonstrances of his friends, continually postponed his call to the bar; and in point of fact never was called.

So the years sped by in idleness, and Everope's resources dwindled and dwindled. At little over forty he was without means, and without a profession. He still hung about the inns of court, pitied by the charitable, despised by the worldly wise. His naturally sanguine temper lent him a certain gaiety of heart, which made him popular with some; and as he never plagued people with his embarrassments, he was still able to find companions. He had been one of Travers's early pupils, and he occasionally looked in at his chambers even yet, although it must be owned very far from a welcome guest.

But he had reached the end of his tether. One might fancy him going wistfully round and round, straining his chain to nibble at some distasteful weed, eagerly pursuing any waif or stray wafted within his circle by the wind, not yet showing his straits by the poorness of his coat, still able to raise a laugh by some eccentricity, but with the lustre of his eyes sadly dimmed, and the confidence of his bearing wofully abated. "When things come to the worst, they must mend," he had been wont to say, forgetting that things never do come to the worst on this side the grave. And now, sanguine still, he clung to hope in the midst of despair, and trusted to chance to retrieve his ruin. It is one of the evils of a course like his, that by the time it is run, the energy which might have shaped a new one is lost, and the self-deluded victim falls, too probably never again to rise. And then is such a course most miserable, when its slave is aware of his own degradation, repents and sins on, always harassed by self-contempt, never safe in self-reliance, always thinking of what he might have been, never remembering what he yet may be.

Men in Everope's condition have but little option in selecting their acquaintance, and often find the embarrassments they cannot uniformly conceal, embolden intrusion, which they would gladly avoid, but are unable to repel. So when Sinson made some advances towards him, the spendthrift intuitively hated, yet silently endured them. And now Michael determined, if possible, to make Everope his bondman.

He had lost no time in fulfilling Mrs. Pendarrel's behest, and found little difficulty in tracing *Morton* to the pleader's chambers. He had not obtained an opportunity of seeing him, but felt certain that the student was no other than Trevethlan. He recollected that Everope had some connection with the law, and might be of service in the schemes which fluctuated indistinctly in his mind. He sought the gambler at the Argyll Rooms.

And he was not disappointed. He saw the wretched man's last guinea swept away by the ruthless rake, and met him as he rose from the table, pale and desperate. "Fortune's a jade, sir," Sinson said, "come and drink a glass of champagne." Everope, scarcely knowing what he did, accepted the invitation, and quaffed glass after glass of the fluid which promised him a temporary oblivion of his plight. He undoubtedly achieved this object, and was unable to resist when his entertainer undertook to see him home. He was, however, sensible enough to be surprised when Sinson followed him into his chambers.

"You are a cool fellow," he stammered. "This is not exactly a palace. I'll get a light, that is if there's a match, and then you can spy the nakedness of the land. Hang me, if you don't look like a spy."

Michael answered by producing a flask. The spendthrift's eyes glistened, and with some trouble he discovered a couple of glasses.

"It is reversing the order of things," he muttered, "reversing the order of things. But no matter. Sufficient for the day—"

As they continued to converse, Everope's contempt for his companion, slid gradually into familiarity. At length the latter, after glancing round the room, exclaimed:—

"Egad! Everope, I guess you're not in arrears for rent?"

"Why so, sir?" asked the spendthrift, with a return of his distant manner.

"Why, there's nothing to levy."

Everope laughed, and dismal it was to hear.

"Clients are few," suggested Sinson, ignorantly.

No answer.

"Family unfriendly," continued the intruder.

"Family!" shouted Everope, springing to his feet with an oath, "what d'ye mean, sir?" He clenched his fist, but it fell to his side. "Ha!" said he, "I am feeble —

'Some undone widow sits upon my arm, And takes away the use o't; and my sword, Glued to my scabbard with wronged orphans' tears, Will not be drawn.'

Kean, sir, Kean——" He sank into his chair, and burst into tears.

This paroxysm restored him to some degree of recollection. When it passed away, Sinson drew his chair near him, and laid his hand on his arm. The spendthrift shrank from the touch. Michael quietly took out his purse, and allowed some pieces of gold to roll on the table.

"Mr. Everope," said he, in the oiliest tones possible, "I ask your pardon for my impertinent intrusion. It was meant all in good will. I was sorry to see the scurvy tricks fortune played you to-night. I came to ask if this petty sum would be any accommodation."

"Sir," Everope answered, while his fingers twitched convulsively, "I do not take such accommodation from strangers."

"We need not be strangers," said Sinson. "And if you are so delicate, you can give me your note of hand. I assure you I do not want the trifle."

Everope looked about the room.

"By the way," continued the tempter, "there's a fellow in the Temple called Morton. Pupil of a Mr. Travers. Know him?"

"I may have seen him at Travers's," the spendthrift answered, sullenly.

"I wish you could find out who he is," Sinson said, "and what he's doing. I have a sort of interest in him."

Everope only continued searching about the apartment.

"Was it paper you were looking for?" Sinson asked, and tore a leaf from his pocket-book.

I O U wrote Everope.

It requires no parchment and blood now-a-days to sign a compact with the fiend.

"Good-night, Everope," said Michael, folding the note in his book. "Recollect what I said about Morton."

The spendthrift closed his door, and returned to the table, and sat down and played mechanically with the golden counters. Embarrassed as he had often been, he had not yet learnt the ways and means of raising money, and this was his initiation. Miserable man! Better for him had it been to submit to any usury than, with his weak temper, to become the debtor of Michael Sinson.

His vacillation was remarkably shown the following day. He rose at a late hour, nervous and feverish, strangely troubled with an idea that he had sold himself to be the instrument of some villany. He knew nothing of the man who had furnished him with money. He could not even tell where to find him. What were his designs with regard to Morton? The little Everope had seen of the young student had won his respect. Ought he not to tell him what had occurred? If he knew where to find this Sinson, he would return the money.

It was dusk of the evening. He remembered that Morton would be keeping Hilary Term. He did not belong to the Temple, but he lived there. He went down into the cloisters and paced to and fro, waiting till hall should be over. At length Randolph came out alone, and Everope joined him abruptly.

"Morton," the spendthrift asked, in a low, husky voice, "were you ever in want?"

The owner of Trevethlan Castle was amazed and affronted, but he said nothing. Since the visit to the opera, every hour made him more impatient of his disguise.

"I ask you were you ever in want?" repeated Everope, with some fierceness. "I do not mean did you ever need a meal, or lack a coat; but were you ever embarrassed? Were you ever afraid, or ashamed to show your face? Did you ever tremble to think, not perhaps of to-morrow, but of to-morrow month? Did you ever shudder at the thought of disgrace? Have you any relatives whom you esteem and love? Whose memory has been to some extent your guardian angel? who have begun to pity and ceased to regard you? To whom you have done injustice? Ay, hark in your ear,—did you ever think that to them your death would be a relief?"

"Is the man mad?" Randolph asked himself, but said nothing aloud.

"I see," continued Everope, gloomily; "I see you are more fortunate. You have no sympathy with a vaurien. My confidence is made in vain: for if you cannot answer these questions, I can. You do not know the circumstances which give force to temptation. Pity those who do. Pity me, Morton. Lay up my words, and have a pardon ready when the day comes."

They had reached Fleet-street. The spendthrift turned suddenly and hurried away, before Randolph could fulfil an intention he had conceived of offering assistance. His own mind was at this time so disturbed, that the episode scarcely increased his agitation. Nevertheless, he went the next morning to make the offer, which Everope's abrupt departure had prevented in the evening. The spendthrift lived in garrets looking down from a great height on a narrow dingy lane. The visitor found the outer door closed, "the oak sported," in the language of college. But he had learnt that this by no means proved the absence of the occupant, and he supposed that in Everope's case there might be good reason for the precaution. So he rapped long and loud at the massive door. There was no answer: no sound indicated the presence of any living creature. "Mr. Everope," Randolph shouted through the narrow aperture intended to receive letters. He repeated the call several times. At length a slight shuffling noise came along the passage inside, and paused at the door.

"Is it you, Morton?" the spendthrift asked.

"Yes. I wish to speak with you."

"Excuse me," said Everope; "I am not well. I cannot see you now. My head aches."

"Nay," Randolph urged, in a low tone. "Only for a moment. Can I be of service to you? I am not rich, but perhaps——From what you said, I thought——"

A sigh, so profound that it might be termed a groan, escaped from Everope's breast. But he lashed himself into a spasm of anger.

"You mistook me, sir," he said, savagely, "and you trouble me. I can hear no more."

And he went back from the door with a quick and heavy tread. He had been to the rooms again the night before, had lost all he borrowed, and accepted a fresh loan from Sinson. It is but the first step that costs.

Randolph betook himself to chambers with a notion that he did not engross all the misery of the world.

———

CHAPTER XI.

There's a dark spirit walking in our house,
And swiftly will the Destiny close on us.
It drove me hither from my calm asylum,
It mocks my soul with charming witchery,
It lures me forward in a seraph's shape.
I see it near, I see it nearer floating,
It draws, it pulls me with a godlike power—
And lo, the abyss.

COLERIDGE. *Piccolomini.*

It would be difficult adequately to portray the conflict of emotions which now agitated our hero. His life at Trevethlan Castle might be described as a long childhood, and the boy became a man at one bound, instead of by insensible degrees. Hence he had not learned to control his sensations. He was driven about by every wind. His will was almost passive. No master-feeling yet called it into action. We have seen how keenly alive he was to the want of that deference which he considered his due; how his pride revolted from the familiarity of those around him; how his feigned name continually irritated him. And all these feelings were embittered by the visit to the opera. Often afterwards he remembered the dark presentiment which oppressed him during the gloomy ride, and which returned while he gazed, rapt in ecstasy, on that fair vision near him, on Mildred Pendarrel. In her he recognised the image which of late years haunted his dreams by the sea; the heroine of the romances which his fancy created; the mistress of his enchanted castle. She was the object for which he had been secretly yearning; the being destined to fill a void which had opened in his existence; the woman for whom he would live and die. In the first few moments he looked at her, his eyes drank in a deep draught of love, and he was hers for ever.

He revelled in the new passion. In those few moments he lived an age. What face was that which intervened between him and his love? Where had he seen those proud lineaments? He required no hint from Helen to remind him of the miniature. He recognised his father's Esther at a glance; he sprang to the conclusion that it was her daughter he adored; and he remembered the vow that lay upon his soul. What wonder that he should feel a presentiment of ill?

There are those who smile when they hear of "love at first sight." But he who drew Romeo was better versed in the heart of man. Such love is a more turbulent and consuming passion than the happier affection which grows up by gentle steps. Swift as the lightning, it is also as desolating. Hope cherishes the softer emotion; hopelessness often seems to fan the more sudden fire.

The first effect of his new passion upon Randolph was to give tenfold vigour to his hatred of his assumed name. Of right, he was Mildred's equal. Even studying for his profession as Randolph Trevethlan, he would still be her equal. But as the obscure pretender, Morton, he was degraded far beneath her. In his proper person, he could surmount all obstacles to obtain her. Could he? What, then, became of his vow?

That very pledge he had given in exchange for permission to wear the detested mask. What a web he had spun around himself! And should he break it at once? Should he dash boldly into the world in his own name, sweep impediments from before him, woo Mildred in spite of everything, and bear her off to his ancestral towers, ay, in defiance of her haughty mother? Would it not be a revenge acceptable to the shade of his broken-hearted father?

His wavering irresolution made him fretful, and almost morose. It caused also a strange craving for excitement. He became impatient of his quiet evenings at Hampstead. It was ungrateful, but he could not help it. Helen saw his irritation with sorrow, but without complaint. Rereworth saw it, and tried vainly to soothe it. He had frequently pressed Randolph to accompany him into society; he prevailed on him to acquire the accomplishments of life, and thereby provided a considerable source of amusement for Mr. Peach, who frequently inquired concerning his lodger's progress in the airs and graces.

"My dancing!" Randolph might exclaim in answer to such queries; "it prospers marvellously. Yet methinks it is a ridiculous occupation."

"By no means, my dear sir," would be the reply. "Hath not the 'Spectator' observed, that 'no one was ever a good dancer that had not a good understanding?' Ah! I see why you smile; but that's not the meaning."

But hitherto Rereworth had been unable to persuade his friend to avail himself of his new acquirements. Trevethlan's secret held him back. It met him at every turn. But now, in his eagerness to forget himself, he at last consented to go with Seymour to an assembly at the house of a near relation, where, Rereworth said, his friends were always welcome. The evening arrived, and Randolph joined his introducer at his chambers.

"You may call yourself a happy man, Morton," cried Rereworth gaily. "You shall be the envy of all our sex, for my fair cousin's sister is the loveliest girl in London, and I have made her promise to be disengaged to dance with you. I told her you were a very good-looking fellow."

"That is not a good introduction," Randolph said, with a faint smile. "But you sacrifice yourself."

"Never fear, you won't disappoint her," Seymour continued. "And as for me, I have romped with her this many a day. She waltzes with me in the morning, and teazes me in the evening. I shall really be glad to inflict her upon you."

"Then I accept the doom," said Randolph.

"Dance with her after supper," added his friend. "That's the time when 'beauty like the midnight flower—'" and Rereworth whistled "Fly not yet."

His companion's spirits rose under the influence of his own.

"Another glass to her health, Morton, and let us away."

It was quaffed, and they departed. A lumbering hackney-coach conveyed them to Cavendish-square. "Mr. Rereworth." ... "Mr. Rereworth." And Randolph had made his bow to Mrs. Winston.

It is not easy for one who went down his first country-dance when seven years old, at a children's ball, and has since practised the festive science until he is too old to obtain any but children for partners, to imagine the sensations of a novice like Randolph. Leaning on Rereworth's arm, he looked confusedly at the fluctuating scene around him, stationary himself among a universal motion, silent amidst an all-pervading voice. His friend in the meantime was surveying the company as it flowed tranquilly by him, recognising acquaintances, now and then exchanging a few sentences. Randolph heeded him not, being engaged in a fanciful comparison of the assembly to the sea, and blending the faces of the company into waves, instead of distinguishing individuals. He did not even observe that one quitted the stream and ranged itself on the other side of Rereworth. He did not observe it, until that gentleman, pressing his arm, said, "Morton, my cousin-*in-law*, Miss Pendarrel."

It was a little sudden. Schoolboys tell stories about home and relations; "men" at college become more reserved; in the world such confidences cease. One sometimes knows nothing even of an intimate friend's family. Thus Rereworth had not mentioned other names in his invitation to Randolph, and Winston brought no associations to his mind at its first announcement. But the case was very different when he heard that of Pendarrel, and recognised its fair owner.

Mechanically, intuitively, he offered Mildred his arm. She laid her hand lightly within it, and they moved onward with the crowd. They made the tour of the saloon before the cavalier uttered a syllable. "Seymour has brought me an oddity," thought Mildred. Randolph was overwhelmed with a flood of rapid emotions, sombre as the canopy which hung above his father's deathbed. His heart beat quick, and he pressed his lips together, struggling hard to obtain a mastery over the tumult within him. One moment he wished he could vanish away, the next he thrilled with rapture at the light touch upon his arm. Mildred was perplexed. She knew she might esteem any one of whom Rereworth spoke well. She had been prepared to see, and to excuse, a little confusion. But there was more here than the confusion of a novice.

"Pardon me, Miss Pendarrel," at length Randolph said, in a voice of tremulous tenderness: "I am new and strange to society. I have relied too lightly on my friend's promises. I walk in a dream."

There is a sort of seeming egotism which is very profitable in love. Few men will fail to excite interest by the true account of their own emotions. To a woman the confidence is always flattering. Randolph's speech was strangely at variance with the usual persiflage. But, perhaps, if he had intended to make love, he could not have spoken better. Mildred was struck by his accent, and interested by his manner. But she was experienced.

"A pleasant dream, Mr. Morton, I hope," she said.

He quivered at the sound of the name.

"Pleasant!" he exclaimed; and then recovering himself partly—"I think it is pleasant.... They are forming quadrilles. Shall we dance, Miss Pendarrel?"

"If you please," answered Mildred, partly puzzled and partly provoked. "Mr. Melcomb," she added to that gentleman, as he passed with a lady, "you will be my *vis-à-vis*."

Melcomb bowed, looked at Mildred's partner, and raised his eyebrows slightly. Randolph recollected the man he had seen at the opera, disliked what he fancied was a singular familiarity, and wondered what was the coxcomb's position in the family. As he warmed in the dance, however, his moodiness and taciturnity gave way. He flung himself into the humour of the moment, retrieved his character with his partner, and obtained another engagement. "Let destiny decide," he said to himself.

Melcomb was Mildred's partner in the next set.

"Who is your unknown knight?" he asked.

"My partner!" said the lady. "A friend of Mr. Rereworth's."

"He is in love with you," remarked the coxcomb.

"I hope he is," Mildred laughed.

"Cruel! He will languish and die."

"That is as I please. I am to dance with him again."

"Is Mrs. Pendarrel here?"

It was a taunt, and Mildred felt it.

Turn the kaleidoscope. "I consider," wrote Sir Richard Steele, "woman as a beautiful romantic animal, that may be adorned with furs and feathers, pearls and diamonds, ores and silks. The lynx shall cast its skin at her feet to make her a tippet; the peacock, parrot, and swan shall pay contributions to her muff; the sea shall be searched for shells, and the rocks for gems; and every part of nature shall furnish out its share towards the embellishment of a creature that is the most consummate work of it." The numerous fair forms in Mrs. Winston's saloons, on which such adornments were lavished in profusion, might easily remind a spectator of the toy which we have named. Randolph, after resigning his partner, wandered rather desolately through the brilliant throng, unobservant and little observed. Finding a vacant and remote corner, he ensconced himself there as an absentee. The gay crowd glimmered before his eyes with the changing hues of the opal, the music sounded from afar like the waves on the sea-shore. Why did that association continually intrude? Why did the muser's thoughts ever turn to Trevethlan? Why did he wish, so earnestly, ever and anon, that he had never quitted the home of his fathers?

Solitude in a crowd has been the theme of much moralizing. In Randolph's case it was peculiarly striking, for it was due, not merely to absence of mind, but also to an absolute want of acquaintance. Except Rereworth and his late partner, the muser might be said to know no one in the whole of the gay assembly. And even Seymour was ignorant of his real situation. Randolph felt oppressed by his loneliness, yet at the same time unwilling to accept any companionship.

In such mood he was, when a voice pierced through the cloud which surrounded him. Rereworth came to seek his friend.

"Morton," he cried, laughing, "'awake, arise, or be for ever fallen.' Winston desires me to present you. Winston, Mr. Morton—Morton, Mr. Winston. Pray find my friend a partner, most philosophical sir."

But Randolph begged to be excused. He escaped from the metaphysician, found his way to an uncurtained window, and looked forth upon the midnight sky. The stars were shining, and he thought of the science which pretended to connect their aspects with the fate of the wanderers upon earth. Which was his? The planet of the queen of love was there, bright in the deep blue canopy. Was she his friend? It was a soothing idea. He forgot his doubts and presentiments, and allowed himself to indulge in the most delicious dreams. His fancy became exalted to the highest pitch. He felt supremely happy.

In this disposition he sought Mildred to claim her engagement. She could complain of no want of devotion now. Her partner was romantic, without sentimentalism; serious, and yet full of imagination. He was pleased, and he exerted himself to please. He allowed his natural enthusiasm to take its course. Mildred wondered no longer at the praises which Rereworth had bestowed upon his friend.

A quadrille affords but scanty and inconvenient opportunity for conversation. But Randolph managed to protract the subsequent promenade. He even drew Mildred apart to that deserted window from which he had been gazing on the sky, and rehearsed some of the marvels of the astrologers, pointing out the planet which had attracted his attention. But he was suddenly awakened from his entrancement. Mrs. Pendarrel, leaning on Melcomb's arm, came to seek her daughter.

"Mildred, my dear," she said, "I have sent to call our carriage." And she held her arm to the young lady, and bowed very loftily to Randolph.

"The carriage is at the door, my dear," said a little man, bustling up with some officiousness. Randolph had retired a few paces, but not so far as to avoid hearing the first of the following words. It was Esther that spoke.

"Mr. Trevethlan Pendarrel, I should be glad if you would ascertain who that gentleman is. A Mr. Morton, I understand. Hark, sir," she whispered, "do you see no likeness?"

"Yes, my dear, certainly I do," said the obsequious husband. "To whom?"

Randolph advanced at the same moment.

"Spare your pains, sir," he said; "I am Randolph Trevethlan."

Face to face, only two steps apart, with their eyes fixed on each other, stood the son and the lover of Henry Trevethlan. Esther's countenance was inscrutable. Her daughter clung to her arm, with cheeks and forehead flushed crimson, and glanced involuntarily at her late partner. Mr. Pendarrel had shrunk a little behind. Melcomb showed a nonchalant dislike to a scene. Randolph faced them, pale as death, his head thrown back, his breast heaving, his eyes flashing fire. But he recovered himself in an instant, bent one look of ineffable tenderness on Mildred, and rushed from the house.

CHAPTER XII.

Disguise, I see thou art a wickedness,
Wherein the pregnant enemy does much.

SHAKSPEARE.

There was no sleep for Randolph that night. One moment had dissipated all the dreams of his youth. One word had dissolved the airy castle. Henceforth he was Trevethlan. So sudden a change, brought about in such a manner, could not but cause great agitation, yet in the midst of all his tumultuous reflections Randolph felt a secret satisfaction. He exulted in the resumption of his name; he felt an energy developing itself within him, very opposite in character to the irresolution which for some time had paralyzed his will. Yet he was saddened by the thought of the sister who had cheered his way, and encouraged his progress. Happy, say we with the good chaplain of Trevethlan Castle, happy is the man who, in the days of his apprenticeship to the world, after he has quitted the home of his youth, and before he has founded a home of his own, has a sister to share his dwelling, and save him from the miserable existence of a young bachelor. Happy is he who has a smile ever ready to welcome him to his fireside, to cheer his evening, and protect him from himself. What talents had not been squandered, what evil had been averted, what ruin prevented, by such companionship! No one cause, perhaps, has wrecked so many fair hopes and promises as the want of a home.

Helen saw a marked change in her brother's countenance when they met for breakfast. The anxiety she had long noticed with regret had vanished, and was succeeded by an air of grave determination. She asked him a few questions concerning the party, but finding him absent and taciturn, soon desisted. Pleasure gleamed in her eyes, however, when, in answer to Mr. Peach, who put his head in at the door to inquire if Randolph would accompany him to town, the latter thanked him, and declined.

"And quite right, my good sir," said Cornelius, advancing into the room. "What saith Marsilius Ficinus, one of old Burton's quaint physicians? 'Other men look to their tools; a painter will wash his pencils, a smith take heed to his forge, and a husband-man to his plough; a falconer and a huntsman care for their hawks and hounds; only scholars neglect that instrument—their brain and spirits, I mean—which they daily use, and by which they range over all the world, but which by much study is consumed.' But I protest—I beg pardon—and hark! there's the stage. Good-morning, Miss Morton—good-morning."

And with several bows he bustled out of the little parlour.

"A kind-hearted creature," observed Randolph, "as ever breathed. I should like to bring him and our Polydore together. They would quite love one another."

Helen had smiled at her brother's idea, before she noticed the gravity with which he spoke. She then looked somewhat disturbed. In spite of all Randolph's care, she had partly suspected the cause of his solicitude, and had consulted Mr. Riches on the subject, suggesting also that it might be well if they could visit Trevethlan in the spring. The chaplain's answer had only arrived the preceding day. There was a certain quaintness about it characteristic of the writer.

"My dear Helen," Polydore said—"your letter has warmed the heart of your old master. I am proud that you should seek my advice, and prouder that you so little need it. The disguise wrong? Surely I think not. By what shall our actions be judged but by our motives? Always provided that we do not evil that good may come. Of the worthiness of your motive there can be no question. Is there anything unworthy in the means? Surely, I say, I think not. When the daw dresses himself in the peacock's plumage, we laugh and despise him, if it is from vanity; we frown and strip him, if it is for deceit. So the wolf cannot assume the sheep's clothing without treachery, nor can the ass wear the lion's skin without contempt. So, again, I prefer Alfred neglecting the neatherd's cakes, to Alfred harping in the camp of the Danes. A king may work with honour in a shipwright's yard, but a king should not condescend to become a spy. "Yet is disguise always an awkward thing. Concealment is repugnant to a candid mind. I like it not myself, and I appreciate the scruples you attribute to Randolph. I had rather you were Trevethlans to the world, as to me. But he thinks himself precluded. We will not dwell upon that. He must be idle, or he must labour under a veil. What abstract harm is there in the metamorphosis? Whom does it wrong? Ah, my dear Helen, I fear I am becoming entangled in sophisms: the path which appeared so direct when I began to write, already seems devious and difficult. To your own conscience, and to Him who directs it, I must leave you, confident that under His guidance you can never go astray. "But I am warranted in cautioning you against a rash judgment. You have delighted me, and not only me, but also our friend Griffith, and his good helpmate, with the proposal, if it be feasible, of a vernal visit. Thereanent have we held a council; and we decide that it can be done, and saving respect, shall be done. Oh! how I long for the day! But that is not what I was about to say. Oh! yes. Postpone until then our deliberations. Let Randolph become versed in the mysteries of his craft. And when you are here, we will plead the cause in form, to rejoinder and sur-rejoinder, rebutter and sur-rebutter. Above all, we will have dilatory pleas in favour of remaining at Trevethlan. You see I have been taking lessons—ahem! "Little news at Trevethlan: not good that little. The miners still disturbed: troops located here and there: rumours very frequent. Our Jeffrey has strengthened the defences of the castle, and sleeps, or wakes, with a loaded blunderbuss. He has consulted me as to whether the cannon on the battlements are safe to fire. And worse, Edward Owen, of our own village, is said to be much with the disaffected. The gossips report, he frets for Mercy Page. And the pretty Mercy frets too, for she has lost her sweetheart. I wish she would not discompose Owen. In the castle we are all quite well, and every one commends himself or herself to you. "May Heaven bless you, and so farewell!

"POLYDORE RICHES."

There was an indecision in this letter, which made Helen unwilling to show it to her brother immediately. She was very far from imagining how completely all its intentions were already superseded. She now anxiously awaited an explanation of the grave expression of Randolph's countenance.

"Sister," he said, "my own sister, it is all over. The bubble has burst. We return immediately to Trevethlan."

"Home!" Helen exclaimed, displaying, both in voice and mien, the most lively astonishment, "What change is this, Randolph?"

"You remember the lady we saw at the opera," the brother said rapidly. "The miniature—the wife of Philip Pendarrel. I encountered her last night, heard her desire her husband to learn who I was, saved him the trouble, confronting her, and announcing my name—Randolph Trevethlan."

There was a short silence. Then the speaker resumed.

"Thank Heaven! I am free. Free from that double-faced servitude. I can look men in the face without fear or shame. I am firm on my feet, let the tempest howl round me as it will. Dearest," he continued folding his sister to his bosom, "pardon me for thus sudden rupture of all our hopes. We will forget them, or think of them as a chapter of romance."

"Is it inevitable?" Helen asked in a low tone.

"Ay," Randolph answered. "The disguise has led me to the brink of an abyss. Even now I know not whether I have recoiled in time. Forgive me, I am scarcely calm. One day I may tell you more. But let us for ever shake off this degrading masquerade. We will go home to Trevethlan. Will you not like to see the sea beating at our feet? It is vain to regret. Ah, me! It is hopeless to forget."

Peremptoriness and fondness mingled both in his word and manner. He kissed his sister's cheek.

"Write, dearest, to Polydore," he continued. "The news will make him sad. You will soften it better than I. Say, we will be at home immediately after the letter. For myself, I have much to do."

Helen obeyed, with many a thought of the surprise which her letter would occasion, coming so close upon that communication of the chaplain's, which the reader has just perused. And Randolph drew up a memorial to the benchers of his Inn, in which he very briefly stated the case, and petitioned for the removal of his name from their books, a matter of course. With this he proceeded to town, and delivered it at the proper office. He then called upon Rereworth. His friend had not yet heard of the scene at Mrs. Winston's.

"Rereworth," he said, "I have a tale to tell you, and an apology to make. Let it be done in the fresh air. Come with me into the gardens."

So they went down into those pleasant grounds, rife with historical recollections, and not long previously the field of exercise for that regiment of legal volunteers, which ambiguous wit designated "the devil's own." May we never see a year like eighteen hundred and eleven!

"You little thought," said Randolph, as they paced the terrace by the Thames, "that in presenting me to Mrs. Winston last night, you introduced a relation."

Rereworth turned and looked at the speaker with unfeigned surprise.

"Under the name of Winston," the latter continued, "I did not recognize a Pendarrel. I am Randolph Trevethlan. Yes, you may well show astonishment. But bear with me a moment. No mean purpose lurked under my masquerade.

"You know that the last owner of Trevethlan Castle had long lost the means of maintaining his house. I inherited a ruin and a name. To restore the one, without degrading the other, was the hope of my life. Doubtless the supposed retreat to the continent, of my sister and myself, was attributed to motives of economy. But we had a very different object in view. Reared in that lonely castle by the sea, ignorant of society, enthusiasts perhaps by nature, we taught ourselves to look forward to a renovation of our old splendour, and to my success in a profession as the means. We read of such things in our library. But there was one obstacle. My poor father—a man of much sorrow, Rereworth—had the feelings which—which men often have. With his dying breath he forbade me to risk the fame of his race in such an enterprise. It was then I mentioned the plan I had devised with my sister. The world might suppose us to be sojourning in a strange land, while in fact we stayed here, and I toiled under a feigned name in an honourable profession. With a struggle my father consented to the scheme. Our steward introduced me as Morton to Mr. Winter, and that gentleman procured me admission to the Temple. But the dream has vanished away."

So far Randolph spoke firmly and quickly. But his voice trembled, and his words came more slowly as he proceeded.

"You may know the terms—but it matters not. Mrs. Pendarrel was once acquainted with my father. I suppose she detected a likeness in me. I heard her inquire about me last night. To be Morton in her presence! It was what I could not bear. I avowed my name.—You will yourself excuse the imposition. You will excuse it for me to Mrs. Winston as best you may."

Rereworth's wonder had increased with every word he heard. It was so strange an encroachment on the ordinary monotony of life. He was aware of the quarrel between the late Mr. Trevethlan and Mrs. Pendarrel. He understood the feelings which had prompted Randolph. He regretted the termination of his career. It was the last sentiment that he expressed in his answer.

"Trevethlan," he said, "no apology will be necessary. Forgive me, if I grieve that your intentions should be defeated. For you may know that this makes your admission here void. But believe me, my regard was not for your name, and will be unaltered."

"I care for nothing else," said Randolph. "Already I have petitioned the bench. My sister and I return to Cornwall directly. Since you are so kind, perhaps you will spend the evening with us."

Rereworth consented, and his friend left him musing in the gardens. This then was the romance which surrounded the brother and sister, and the solution of the peculiarities upon which he had often meditated. The form of Helen Trevethlan stole gently into his reverie, not unwelcome. He was sorry to think she was going away, but at the same time glad that he was to see her again before she left. He pondered on the family feud, which was nothing to him—his relationship being with the Winstons—and gratified himself with the idea that he might possibly have prepared the way to a reconciliation. So ignorant was he of the true state of the case. But his thoughts continually reverted to the dark eyes of Randolph's sister. He was himself on the point of being called to the bar, having completed his course of preparation, and he asked himself whether a house and a wife would not be agreeable possessions.

Meantime his friend went and discovered himself to Mr. Winter. The lawyer was much annoyed, and looked very grave.

"I will not conceal from you, Mr. Trevethlan, since so I must call you," he said, after some reflection, "that your story gives me great dissatisfaction. It is only a blunder, but I wish my old friend Griffith had consulted me before sanctioning this scheme, and implicating me in it."

Randolph protested that the blame was imputable solely to himself.

"I know," said the lawyer, "I know all you would say. I am not attributing any fault to anybody. But I am vexed. I thought Griffith was more a man of the world. As for the worthy chaplain, parsons are seldom men of business. But I wish my old friend had confided in me."

"It was my fault he did not," said Randolph.

"In truth," Winter observed, "now I know all this, I am surprised I did not suspect it before, for you have the family countenance perfectly, Mr. Trevethlan. I know it well. And so has your sister. It is wonderful I did not think of it."

The conversation diverged to family affairs, and gloomy enough seemed the fortunes of the house of Trevethlan. At length Randolph took his leave, having informed the lawyer of his immediate departure for Cornwall.

The activity and vigour with which he fulfilled his resolution diverted his thoughts from the flame which burned hotly within him and indeed inspired his energy. But, in fact, although he did not know it, he was nearly desperate. He might have felt his own impatience while Winter was speaking to him. And as he walked alone through the fields, on his way back to Hampstead, the consciousness of his passion revived.

"She is mine," he almost muttered aloud—"mine by every right. Family ties, family feuds, parent's commands, social conventionalities, they are cobwebs under my hand. She has robbed me of my life; she must give me herself in exchange. I would die for her; she must live for me. I go to my home to feel myself a Trevethlan. I shall breathe the air of my native halls; I shall catch the inspiration of my race; I shall come forth to trample on form and rule, and to bear off my bride in defiance of the world. Look to your house, Esther Pendarrel. The bars are unbroken, the locks are unforced. Where is your child? In the castle by the sea. Weep, proud woman—weep and rend your hair for her who shall never return! Was it not enough to destroy the father, but the son also must be crushed? But I am made of sterner stuff. The heel will be bruised that tramples me. I will not play the game of my foe. Look to your house. Did the watchman slumber? Who shall watch love? The wind of midnight bore her the message, and she fled. The bird sang on the house-top, and she heard the song. The stars of heaven, ay, that star we looked upon last night, summoned her away. Fasten your windows, muster your guards, note her downsitting and her uprising. What! is her place empty? Search highest and lowest. Gone? Yes, she is mine! she is mine!"

There was a softening influence in the conviction, wildly as it was expressed. Randolph's exaltation subsided as he became intimately persuaded that his passion must have a happy issue, in spite of the difficulties which seemed to threaten its course, and he was calm and collected when he arrived at his dwelling and joined his sister. But he was anxious for action, motion—anything but repose—and it was agreed that they should depart the very next day.

Rereworth came to them, according to his engagement, some time before sun-set, and, as it was a fine genial evening, they strolled to the fields above West End, and looked on the pleasant landscape, so agreeably described by the author of the 'Sketch Book,' "with its soft bosom of green pasturage lying open to the south, and dotted with cattle; the steeple of Hampstead rising among rich groves on the brow of the hill; and the learned height of Harrow in the distance." Even at this dull season, though the trees were leafless and the hedges bare, the prospect was not without its beauties; and Rereworth discoursed of them to Helen in a manner which, to him at least, was particularly interesting.

For some time they had the conversation—rather serious it was—to themselves; Randolph taking no part. But when it diverged to the opera, and from thence to the preternatural drama, and from thence to what Madame de Staël termed the *côté nocturne de la nature*, he suddenly exclaimed:

"There is a strange fascination in these things. Presentiments seem to be so often fulfilled."

"Because," Rereworth said, "they are generally felt where the result is probable. What was more likely than that Henri Quatre should die by the dagger of an assassin? These pretended second-sights, of all kinds, must, in fact, be revelations. And to admit their truth, is to depreciate the value of Revelation. I explain the whole thing with four lines from Wordsworth:

'What strange and wayward thoughts will slide
Into a lover's head! Ah, mercy! to myself I cried,
If Lucy should be dead!'"

"And suppose Lucy's wraith flitted by at the moment," said Helen, smiling.

"All in white, uncommonly like a shred of mist," added Rereworth.

"Yet," Randolph urged, "there is something very picturesque in these superstitions, if such they must be called."

"Certainly," said his friend. "I enjoy them, but I do not believe them. I enjoy them more than those who believe and tremble. I love a good legend, or even a well-invented modern tale of gramarye."

"We shall all be mystified by the author of 'Waverley,'" Helen said. "Already we have had Fergus's strange monitor, and the fortune told for Henry Bertram, and the Ravenswood prophecy, every one of them verified in the event."

"The constant return to such machinery," remarked Randolph, "shows how readily it finds belief."

"It is continually supported by coincidences," Rereworth answered. "Under striking circumstances, a man dreams of his absent friend. On the same night the latter dies. Granted in all the fulness of mystery. Now how many people were in the same relative position at the same time? How many dreamt or fancied the same thing? Hundreds? Thousands? Ay,—tens of thousands. Out of myriads of dreams one is verified. It proves the baselessness of the fabric."

"One never hears of the dreams which do not come true," observed Helen.

"No, Miss Trevethlan," Seymour said. "These visions and the sayings of fortune-tellers are tentative; like those famous miracles, the stoppage of which occasioned the well-known epigram—

'De par le roi, defense à Dieu, De faire miracle en ce lieu.'"

"There is an old dame, not far from us in the country," said Helen, "who I have heard, has threatened a violent death to half Penwith."

"Dismal individual!" exclaimed Rereworth.

"Our host complains," Helen continued, "of the decay of these old wonders. There's not a child in Hampstead, he says, but will cross the churchyard by night."

"Ay," said Randolph, "the age is incredulous. For my part, I should like to be a visionary."

Helen perceived that her brother spoke rather moodily.

"The sun is setting," she said. "If we stay much longer, we shall have it dark enough to encounter some spectre ourselves. Let us go home."

So they went. Rereworth lingered with them as long as he could, thinking of the distance which would soon divide him from Helen. Should they ever meet again? He felt that it only rested with himself to strengthen the favourable impression he had already made. But would not absence efface it? It was a question which must be left to time. He was not certain of his own feelings. He had arranged a correspondence with Randolph. He should therefore at least hear of Helen. He fancied there was an unusual gloominess in his chambers that night. The fire was out; and when he lighted his lamp, the dark wainscotting of the walls, which he used to admire, wore a sombre appearance. He retired to rest and dreamt of Trevethlan Castle.

The orphans thought it unnecessary to reveal themselves to their good host and hostess. They merely said that circumstances called them suddenly home. They had but few adieus to make, trifling matters to settle, little baggage to pack. Cornelius and his sister had become attached to their lodgers, and parted with them with more than ordinary regret. Mr. Peach expressed his grief that they had come to Hampstead late in the fall and quitted it before the Spring. They knew not the beauties of his favourite suburb. His even cheerfulness was shaded for a moment; he was reminded that he had a side to the wall. He insisted on accompanying his young friends to the ancient inn from which they were to start. And strange humours thronged upon his fancy, while he stood in the court of the old-fashioned hostelry, when the rattling mail had departed, looked up at the fantastic open galleries, and peopled them with the guests of by-gone days. He went up to Hampstead in a mood more serious than his wont; smoked his pipe tranquilly a long time, while Clotilda sat knitting him a comforter, and finished the evening with a desultory discourse on the beauties and merits of his never-forgotten Mabel.

CHAPTER XIII.

Revenged!
How should I be revenged? If this be true,
As I have such a heart, that both mine ears
Must not in haste abuse—if it be true,
How should I be revenged?

SHAKSPEARE.

The emotion experienced by Esther Pendarrel, when the heir of Trevethlan confronted her with the avowal of his name, was by no means of unmitigated animosity. Many a tender recollection arose in her mind, as she gazed, fascinated, upon features so strongly recalling those which, in days long gone, she had stored up in her heart of hearts. The remembrance of her affection prevailed for a moment over her sense of wrong and desire for retribution. But it was only for a moment. She saw the flushed face of her daughter, and the shrinking demeanour of her husband. The first she noted with alarm, the second with disgust. Her feelings recoiled upon the son of her discarded suitor. That he should be an object of interest to her child, and of fear or reproach to her lord, made him the more odious to herself.

"Morton," she might have said in the solitude of her chamber at night— "Randolph Morton! Seeking the fortune so recklessly thrown away! Hoping that the successful advocate would repair the ruin of Trevethlan Castle! And such things are possible. Many a new family dates its origin from the forum. Might not an old one, in like manner, retrieve its fall? But why the feigned name? Was it the old pride? Oh, Henry, Henry Trevethlan! that pride has brought desolation to thee and to me—to thine, and, perhaps, to mine. Was there not passion in those burning cheeks, and in that quivering arm?

"And so we are face to face. Foes, irreconcileable, to war to the death. What was the dark hint which flashed across my mind? Who said there was no marriage?"

When Michael Sinson first let fall the insinuation which here rose to the mind of his patroness, the natural generosity of her disposition revolted from the suggestion. But it recurred again and again. There was strong temptation in the idea which it excited. Were it true, at one swoop that peasant woman, whom Mrs. Pendarrel had learned to hate, would be shamed, her son and daughter would be fatherless in an odious sense, their inheritance would be forfeited, and would fall to Esther's family. The children of her lover would be outcasts upon earth. Retribution so full and complete was more than she had ever deemed possible, and continually presented itself to her thoughts, whether she would or no. Sometimes she asked herself, was it not her duty to investigate the matter? did not justice to her own children require it? might she not be charged with allowing them to be defrauded? Besides, supposing the tale was well founded, and her husband's title maintained, and possession had of the castle, there would then be ample opportunity for generosity. But justice should come first. Such were the ideas which had forced themselves upon Mrs. Pendarrel's notice, and been less and less unwelcome, before the meeting at Mrs. Winston's party. The discovery there made gave them a new colouring. If the orphans had chosen to fling aside their name, a name to which they might have no right, need she be scrupulous in scrutinizing their title, and overthrowing it if she could? No, no. Let them be Mortons, or Bassets, or what they would: if they cared so little for the name of Trevethlan who were its natural upholders, surely neither need she who was pledged for its extinction.

The next day Mrs. Pendarrel desired the presence of her protégé. The interview which ensued was long. By dexterous questions, flung out with great apparent nonchalance, and exhibiting a scornful disbelief in the things inquired of, the lady extracted from Michael Sinson all the popular rumours upon which he had founded his insinuation. But if she supposed that her manner blinded him to her real interest, she deceived herself. He was subtile enough to see that the affected indifference was only a disguise. And although, in truth, very willing to unfold his story, he amused himself at times by feigning reluctance, and obliging his patroness to speak more plainly than she desired. The following pages embody the substance of his information, derived, he said, from rumours current in Trevethlan and its neighbourhood when he was a boy, but now nearly forgotten.

Margaret Basset was one of the prettiest girls to be met with between the Lizard and Marazion. Her song was the merriest in the hay-field; her foot was the lightest at Sithney fair. Many a well-to-do young man would have gladly made her his wife, but Margaret was hard to please. And her fastidiousness was not displeasing to her mother, Maud, who was vain of her handsome child, and read a high fortune for her by the *Sortes Apocalypticæ*, to which she had recourse in all matters, both great and small. It was true, that one day, when a strolling gipsy was tempting Margaret to learn her destiny, and Maud rushed out of the house to put the witch to flight, declaring that her girl's fortune required no help from the like of her, the dark woman answered, wrathfully, that what was thought bliss might prove to be bane. But the angry prediction was unheeded at the time, and only remembered when it seemed to be fulfilled by Margaret's premature death.

At that time, Henry Trevethlan was by no means popular among his dependents. He had lately returned to the castle, after a long absence, a ruined man. For a great time the hamlet had derived none of the usual benefits from the residence of its proprietor, and he came home too poor to confer any.

The people were very jealous at the alienation of the family estates, which had so much divided the tenantry. It seemed not unlikely that the prophecy, respecting the union of Trevethlan and Pendarrel, would be verified in a sense far from flattering to the inhabitants of the former, and even without the match.

So, when it was whispered that Mr. Trevethlan was, in fact, seeking a bride from among themselves, they were irritated rather than conciliated. They wanted a lady of fortune and rank, who might make the castle a scene of hospitality, and be generous to the villagers, as the ladies of Trevethlan had always been wont. The prophecy was quoted with more alarm. Any girl, who was said to have attracted their landlord's notice, was regarded with jealousy and dislike. And some old crones indulged in darker sayings: how there could be but one object in such wedlock, and if there were no olive-branches the vine would be found to wither. Either the marriage would be broken, or the bride would die.

Such was the state of feeling in the hamlet, when Mr. Trevethlan demanded the hand of Margaret Basset. Alone, perhaps, among her neighbours, the maiden's mother received the announcement with joy and pride. She accepted it as the fulfilling of her own prediction. Margaret trembled as she thought of the gipsy's. But, whatever were her feelings, she could not resist the desires of her parent, and the authority of the castle. Her sister, Cecily, was her only confidante. The marriage was settled.

But then came the difficulty as to the performance of the ceremony. Mr. Trevethlan respected the pride of his chaplain, but he resolved to meet no other check of the kind. There was a clergyman, a very young man, seeking to repair his shattered health by a residence on that genial coast, and evidently in no very flourishing circumstances. Him did Mr. Trevethlan induce to celebrate the rite, under a special license, within the walls of the castle. Maud, and a young rustic, named Wyley, were the only witnesses; and the country-folk might well conjecture that a marriage, contracted in so singular, and, to them, in so revolting a manner, was irregular, and might be dissolved. Moreover, it was not entered in the parish register until after the birth of Randolph, and then not in the usual form.

So these circumstances provoked much popular indignation. When Mr. Trevethlan took home his bride all the doors in the hamlet were closed, and no individual was visible on the green. Even Jeffrey's face was shaded with discontent when he threw open the gates; and Mr. and Mrs. Griffith could not avoid displaying a little humiliation in receiving their new mistress. Polydore Riches, alone of the household, met her with a sincere welcome, in which kindness was enforced by pity. Some folks wondered that he remained at the castle. But the chaplain had satisfied his conscience by his protest, and stayed to mitigate a misfortune which he was unable to avert.

The day after the marriage the hamlet was startled by an occurrence, which gave fresh force to the suspicions of the villagers. Mr. Ashton, the clergyman, was missed from his lodgings. He went out the evening of the wedding, as was his habit, to stroll along the cliffs, and he never returned. In much excitement the people made a diligent and immediate search, and on the beach below his haunt they found the body of a man, stripped, and so disfigured, that identification was impossible. It was soon discovered that Wyley, the witness, was also missing from his home, and the comments made on the coincidence were loud and strong.

Advertisements brought forward Mr. Ashton's relations. From them Polydore Riches learnt that his health had been ruined by self-indulgence, and that he was allowed a small stipend on condition of residing in perfect retirement. There seemed to be no very particular concern felt about his fate. The gentleman who came down was unable to recognise the body, so great were the injuries it had received, apparently in falling from the cliff. The coroner's inquest returned an open verdict.

There the matter rested. The mystery had not been explained. There were, however, low whispers, that Will Watch's lugger had run along the shore the night Mr. Ashton was missed, and that the country lanes were alive with active traffic. But if it were so, those who could be explicit on the matter if they chose, found it more expedient to hold their tongues.

For a time the event gave, as has been said, new vigour to the suspicions concerning poor Margaret's marriage. Her mother was the only witness remaining. But when a son and heir was born to Mr. Trevethlan, and there came no formal impeachment of the union, the rumours gradually died away. The peasant-lady, by her meekness and modesty, won the regard of all the inmates of the castle, except—her husband. He exacted, indeed, the utmost deference towards her from others, but treated her himself with cold indifference, and seemed jealous of her influence with her children, even in their cradle. She foresaw what would come, pined away, and died. Her bliss had been her bane.

Michael Sinson said nothing to his patroness of the mode in which Mr. Trevethlan behaved to his wife's relations. He did not tell how bitterly old Maud resented the death of her daughter, nor how his own expulsion from the castle rankled even yet in his heart. But he dwelt with much craft on the singular circumstances of the marriage, and the mysterious disappearance of the evidence; hinted at times, that the rite would have been pronounced a mockery, if its purpose had not been achieved, and suggested, not very indistinctly, that it might yet be proved to have been so in reality.

These hints and inuendos were the main novelties of the story to Mrs. Pendarrel. Of her own knowledge, she recollected the leading facts of the case, and was well aware that, whatever might be the prejudices of the vulgar, there was not the slightest public ground to doubt the perfect formality of the marriage. Moreover, she felt certain, from her acquaintance with Henry Trevethlan's character, that he would never be a party to an artifice like that suggested by Sinson. If there were anything irregular, she was sure it was no fault of his. But there was a confidence in her informant's manner which seemed to intimate that he spoke on no light grounds.

"Sinson," she said, after some consideration, and with an air of the most unreserved frankness, "you know, of course, perfectly well, that if the marriage you have been speaking of were not lawfully contracted, the small estate of Trevethlan would fall, by inheritance, to Mr. Pendarrel. And though I am sure he would be disposed to show every kindness to those who in that case would, by no fault of their own, be holding a false position, still justice to his family would compel him to enforce his claim. And any party contributing by proper means to the establishment of the title would, of course, be liberally rewarded. But an attempt which should simply cause annoyance to Mr. Trevethlan without profiting ourselves, would be equally disagreeable to us. And we should be very far, indeed, from speculating on a mere chance, or using any unfair means. Now, from your manner, you appear to possess, or to fancy you do, some information which may be valuable. For myself, I am no judge of such matters; but Mr. Pendarrel will give you an introduction to our lawyer. He will consider the worth of your intelligence, and you may rely on an adequate remuneration."

But this suggestion in no way squared with Michael's designs. It was not exactly a pecuniary recompense that he desired. The calm and level manner in which Mrs. Pendarrel spoke failed to conceal the strong interest she really felt; and since she alluded with such nonchalant openness to consequences, he would be somewhat more explicit as to means.

"I beg pardon, ma'am," he observed. "I supposed you would think it more important. Certainly, ma'am, it is not for me to meddle. To be sure, I know something; but it may be all wrong, and then, ma'am, it would only annoy Mr. Trevethlan to bring it forward. Besides, would I wish to disturb the good name of my poor relation, although it would be no blame to her? So, ma'am, I might pursue a train I have laid, with your leave; and if it leads to anything, then I could have the introduction. If it comes to nothing, there will be no harm done."

After some fencing, Michael obtained from his patroness a vague authority to continue the researches at which he hinted, and he subsequently extracted a further sanction in letters, by writing to her for instructions. He was playing rather a deep game for a very distant object. In this interview he imagined he gained a point or two, and Mrs. Pendarrel might have detected a gleam of exultation in his sinister eyes, when he quitted her presence at its close. And when he met her daughter in his way through the hall, he glanced at her with an expression which might have amused the young lady, but that she always regarded him with an instinctive antipathy.

The conversation disappointed Mrs. Pendarrel. She had hoped for intelligence of a more definite kind, and placed very little reliance on the expectations held out by her protégé. But now another solicitude engaged her attention. In spite of her own excitement when Randolph confronted her with his name, she had not omitted to notice the agitation of Mildred. She saw the scarlet of her face, and felt the pressure of her trembling arm. She fancied she heard the exclamation—my cousin—escape from her lips. Cousin indeed! she thought. Well it will be if that is all.

She had wielded her rod of iron so long, was so accustomed to entire submission from all connected with her, and so firmly persuaded of the power of her will, that in preparing to settle Mildred—pleasing is the ambiguity of the word—as she had succeeded in doing Gertrude, she forgot or undervalued the point of support, which Mrs. Winston's position enabled her to afford her sister. Right well did the clear-sighted mother know, how bitterly Gertrude repented the day when she exchanged captivity with a heart for liberty without. She knew also that Mrs. Winston would certainly take Mildred's part in resisting an unacceptable match. But the knowledge rather stimulated her love of triumph than occasioned her any dread. Parents seem often apt to visit upon their children their own hardships or misfortunes. The parvenu father thinks he has fully excused narrow-mindedness towards his son by saying—the lad is better off than ever I was. And the mother, whose own marriage, was unhappy, will not seldom be careless of her daughters' comfort in theirs.

Now, Mrs. Pendarrel had for some time decided upon Mildred's lot. Mr. Melcomb was to be the happy man. It was true, he was a gambler and a rake; but it was also true that he was the owner of Tolpeden Park and a large estate thereto appended. It was equally true that he was pretty deeply embarrassed; but the extent of his liabilities had not yet transpired, and the prudent mother supposed that her daughter's fortune would pay off the encumbrances upon the land, and that by stringent settlements it might be kept free in future, and secured for the children. And so her descendants would unite Tolpeden and Pendarrel. But Melcomb was desultory in his addresses, haunted by that fear of a refusal already mentioned. Now, however, that Mrs. Pendarrel felt some uneasiness lest Mildred should fall into other chains, she became anxious to bind her at once in a positive engagement.

The coxcomb was nearly a daily visitor at her house, and always admitted. She took an early opportunity of sounding him more closely than before as to his intentions, and hinted hopes of favour. He replied with a proposal in form. Should esteem himself the happiest of men. Feared he might not be acceptable to Miss Pendarrel. That alone had prevented him from declaring himself long before. Sensible of his unworthiness: prepared to devote his life. To which the mother graciously answered, that she felt highly flattered. That her daughter had been educated too prudently to differ from her parents. He might consider the affair settled. No difficulty could arise in the necessary arrangements. Mildred would be ready to receive him on the following day.

CHAPTER XIV.

Juliet. Is there no pity sitting in the clouds,
That sees into the bottom of my grief?
O, sweet my mother, cast me not away!
Delay this marriage for a month—a week—
Or if you do not, make the bridal bed
In that dim monument where Tybalt lies.

Lady Capulet. Talk not to me, for I'll not speak a word:
Do as thou wilt, for I have done with thee.

SHAKSPEARE.

Randolph had amply compensated, in his second dance with Mildred, for any awkwardness which might have attended his first. Even in this he had ultimately succeeded in interesting his partner, and in the other he excited her enthusiasm. Carried away himself by the fatality which seemed to have brought them together, he discoursed in fervent and glowing language of the mystic science which supposed the destinies of mortals to be written in the sky, and pointed to the planet which he had just before imagined might rule his own. It was not as a believer, not as a votary that he spoke, however, but as a lover. Were it not pleasant, he asked, to fancy that friends far apart might look up to those rolling fires, fancy one another's situation, and thus hold a sympathetic communion,—no matter what distance lay between them? And certain it is, that extravagant and romantic as the idea might seem, Mildred never saw the stars afterwards without remembering the question, gazing round for the bright planet which Randolph showed her, and wondering was he also regarding it.

No marvel if she was more than excited by the scene which followed. To find a relation in him whose rich tones still lingered on her ear, whose burning words were still thrilling in her heart; to see in him the cousin of whom she had scarcely heard, but was prepared to love; the dweller of those desolate towers by the sea which she had so often admired in the rambles of her childhood; to think that all she had heard of him concerned the feud which divided them; to read that feud in the flashing eyes which were fixed upon her mother, and to feel the overwhelming tenderness with which they then bent upon herself,—no marvel surely it was that the warm blood rushed to her cheeks, and she trembled in every nerve, and her lips breathed a recognition of her newfound kinsman.

Nor was it an impression likely to be weakened by reflection. All the associations would rather tend to deepen it. The seclusion from which he must have emerged, the mystery which appeared to surround him now, the consequences of his self-betrayal, combined to the same end. Then, too, he had a sister. Was she like him? Where was she abiding? What were her pursuits? Mere curiosity would have found ample employment for reverie, even if no deeper and fonder interest were at hand to protract it.

In such meditations was Mildred absorbed when her mother came to inform her, with stately calmness, that Mr. Melcomb had made a formal demand of her hand; that the offer was highly acceptable to herself and to Mr. Pendarrel, and that her suitor would pay his respects to her the next day. As soon as Mildred had recovered some composure, after the short scene which followed, she threw on her bonnet,—at least she was not yet a prisoner in the house,—and walked to Cavendish-square. Mrs. Winston read the anxiety of her mind at one glance.

"Mildred, dearest," she exclaimed, "what is the matter?—what has happened?"

"Do you recollect," her sister inquired in turn, with a short scornful laugh which Gertrude did not like, "what we said of Mr. Melcomb some time ago? Well, it seems I am to marry him:—that is what's the matter."

"Marry Melcomb! Not while I have a home to offer you," Mrs. Winston said, hastily. "That is, not against your wishes, dear. You may learn to like the man. He is said to have very winning ways."

"Gertrude, Gertrude! do not jest. But we may be interrupted...."

"Come with me, little timidity. Fanchon shall tell them I am not at home." Mrs. Winston led her sister to her boudoir. "Now, dear, talk to me and the mice. You can sit with your back to me if you like."

"Oh, Gertrude, I think my heart will break!"

"Of course, dear. Quite correct."

"Nay, listen, sister," Mildred remonstrated. "I was sitting this morning, doing nothing, thinking, thinking of ... when mamma came suddenly into my room. I was quite startled. Mamma was looking half merry and half solemn. You know, Gertrude?"

"I do, dear," said the elder sister, with some bitterness.

"So she began to flatter me in different ways, and said a great many little things that I could really hardly attend to, and something about the admiration ... and then about obedience and duty, and the words seemed to pass over my mind without making any impression. Till at last mamma assumed a very grave look, and said I must be aware of the particular attentions which had been paid me for a great while. There were, indeed, some attentions that I had felt, but not for a great while.... I was confused,

Gertrude, by the tone in which mamma spoke; she seemed to expect an answer. I do not know what I said."

And Mildred here made a pause in her story, after which she proceeded with more animation.

"Mamma did not keep me long in suspense. A gentleman—highly distinguished—neighbour in the country—general favourite—might have married so and so. Could I not guess? I had taken heart. Neighbour! I thought. I considered the geography of Pendarrel. Bounded on the east, I said to myself, by Mr. Peristyle, married. On the south, Sir Simon Rogers, who married his dairy-maid, and she is just dead. Dear mamma, I asked, am I to be the second Lady Rogers? She laughed, and bade me guess again. West, thought I, west, between us and the sea! And a romantic idea struck me, that I was to be a peace-offering, and with a wild kind of hope, I exclaimed, surely, mamma, it is not my cousin, Randolph? Gertrude, I wish you had seen our mother's face at that moment."

"I can imagine it," Mrs. Winston said.

"For my part," Mildred continued, "my eyes had filled with tears. After a moment's silence, mamma said, in a tone that froze my heart, 'You began at the wrong end. Mr. Melcomb is your suitor; will be your husband.' Sister, I did not believe it. I fancy I smiled. Mamma went on in the same voice—'Let me have no boarding-school nonsense, Mildred, if you please. Rely on your mother's experience, and imitate your sister's prudence. Mr. Melcomb will wait upon you to-morrow.' It was still some time before I understood. I begged for pity, for delay, for anything. Mamma was very, very stern!"

Mildred threw her arms round Gertrude, and bent her face upon her neck.

"Marry him!" she exclaimed in a whisper—"never!"

"Ay," thought Mrs. Winston, pressing her sister to her bosom, "I said the same. And yet.... But I had no refuge. I was unsupported, and helpless. It is a hard struggle. May it not be avoided? Can we not gain time? If Melcomb had a spark of generosity.... But he is too vain ... and even then our mother.... There is nothing for it but time. Mildred, dearest," she continued aloud, "you need not tremble so. You will not have to accept Mr. Melcomb."

"What mean you?" her sister asked, raising her head.

"Listen: I understand this gentleman, and so, I think, do you. He will not dream of asking your consent. He will take it for granted. Let him—let him till the time comes. It will not be long, but we shall have a chance of avoiding éclat. Tell mamma, that though you are not now favourable to Mr. Melcomb, you cannot refuse to see him, and she will be satisfied. And then we shall have the chapter of accidents on our side."

"Must I do this, Gertrude?" Mildred exclaimed. "There was a time when I was amused with his compliments, Heaven forgive me! But to listen to them now! Encourage him, I never did. He knew I was laughing. Ah me! If I escape this time, I will never flirt again."

"Be not too sure," said Gertrude. "But take your sister's word, no harm will come. And remember, here is your home as a last resort. Come, come," she continued, in answer to a sigh from her sister, "let me take you a drive. You are as pale as Ophelia. But ah, ça ira, ça ira ... do not repeat my revolutionary music to papa."

As the sisters rode along, Mrs. Winston turned the conversation to the scene which had occurred at her late party. She had not seen it, nor indeed had any one save those who were mentioned at the time. She brought the colour into Mildred's cheeks, by alluding with a smile, to her retirement with her partner to that unfrequented little room; and she made her heart beat quick by relating all the circumstances which she had learned from Rereworth, who had duly delivered Randolph's message, and taken the opportunity of extolling the merits of his friend. And Gertrude ended by expressing her deep regret at the continuance of the family disagreement, to which her attention had been specifically drawn for the first time, and her hope that it might be approaching its termination. Every word of the narrative increased the interest which was already warm in Mildred's heart, and made her feel a greater repugnance to receiving Melcomb in the equivocal manner recommended by her sister.

CHAPTER XV.

"Regretter ce qu'on aime est un bien, en comparaison de vivre avec ce que l'on haît."

LA BRUYÈRE.

Mildred's trial was not destined to last long. Her suitor was more impatient than Mrs. Winston predicted. He would, indeed, as she suggested, have willingly continued to accept a vicarious consent, until things had gone so far that his intended bride should be unable to recede. Hitherto he had given her no opportunity for resistance, and now with all his assurance he dreaded to begin. Mildred's indifference was so chilling that his spirits deserted him in her presence. He would have left her free, but for the fear of ridicule, and the need, the pressing need, of her fortune. The time came to make the plunge.

"Miss Pendarrel," Melcomb said, as they sat together in a small drawing-room, "dear Miss Pendarrel, you must be aware how long I have been the most devoted of your servants."

Mildred had acquired the habit of receiving Melcomb's compliments in silence. She said nothing.

"It is true no service could make any man worthy of Miss Pendarrel," the suitor continued; "yet I have been led to hope, unworthy as I am, that mine might not be doomed to be endless. Is it not so, dear Miss Pendarrel?"

"You have been led to hope nothing by me, Mr. Melcomb," Mildred answered, agitated by the unusual embarrassment in his manner.

"Nay," urged the coxcomb, "may I not hope from the position which Miss Pendarrel has permitted me to assume...."

"You have had no permission from me, Mr. Melcomb," said Mildred, interrupting him. She had well prepared herself for the scene, and preserved her spirit, though very much distressed.

"Surely," he continued, "I am not presumptuous in considering it implied."

Mildred was silent. Hers was no case for argument.

"Not presumptuous," Melcomb went on, speaking more rapidly, "in aspiring to the happiness which that permission seemed to promise. Not presumptuous in imploring dear Miss Pendarrel to appoint the time, when anxiety and fidelity may be rewarded with joy, and I may become the most fortunate of men."

"Mr. Melcomb," Mildred said, rising from her chair, and trembling, "I am above pretending to misunderstand you. Have you my mother's ... Does she...."

"It is by Mrs. Pendarrel's leave that I venture," said the coxcomb in his softest manner. "And an early day, dearest Mildred,——"

He made a step as if to take her hand, but she recoiled, and said, in a tone of determination, which Melcomb probably never forgot, "The day will never come."

She turned towards the door, but stopped as though she wished to say something more. Melcomb had anticipated a refusal, but not one so decisive.

"Miss Pendarrel will pardon my expressing surprise...." he began to say. Mildred hastily interrupted him, with faltering words.

"Sir, sir, perhaps it is I should ask your pardon—but you have never—it is the first time—I have had no opportunity—in pity to me, sir, urge these addresses no farther."

She could no longer restrain her tears, and quitted the room, Melcomb making no attempt to detain her.

He was neither surprised, nor mortified, nor even discomposed. It was a check by discovery, long expected and prepared for, by no means checkmate. And he had not lost his queen. The game was by no means desperate. But he wished for time to consider his next move, and left the house without seeing Mrs. Pendarrel.

That lady immediately conjectured what had occurred, and only feared that Mildred might have affronted her suitor to such a degree as to make him abandon his intentions. He had not been very long gone before she sought an explanation from her daughter.

"Mildred, my dear child," she said, "what is the meaning of this? How happens it, that the politest of mankind leaves my house without kissing my hand?"

There was a covert irony in Mrs. Pendarrel's manner, which, against her will, betrayed her own contempt for Melcomb, and at the same time showed her ruthless resolution.

"Mamma," Mildred answered, fixing her reddened eyes on her mother's, "you know."

"Nay, child, I am not a divine. I hope you were not rude to Mr. Melcomb? To your intended husband?"

"I refused him, mamma."

"And why did you not refuse him long ago?" Mrs. Pendarrel asked abruptly.

"He never asked me, mother," answered Mildred, swinging her hand to and fro. "He never asked me. Till just now I have heard nothing from him that I could take as a proposal. How anxiously I have waited for one, God knows."

Mrs. Pendarrel bit her lip.

"It is of no consequence," she said, "you cannot recede without disgrace and shame. If you are prepared to submit to them, I am not. This marriage must proceed. Always, that is, if you have not affronted Mr. Melcomb irrevocably. But you dared not."

A flash in Mildred's eye at the word might show Esther more daring than she would like.

"Mother," she said, "I prayed Mr. Melcomb, in pity, to urge his suit no more. I make a similar prayer to you. And, mother, there is one thing I dare not do. I dare not wed this man."

"I fancy you will find heart," said Mrs. Pendarrel, with a sneer on the word. "And since you are so agitated, you had better stay at home till you do."

But that home was to be changed. Immediately after this conversation, Mrs. Pendarrel determined to carry her daughter down into Cornwall, and finish the matter with a high hand. She had another motive for the journey, having heard from Sinson that the Trevethlans had gone home, and feeling, she scarcely knew why, desirous to be near them. But, before she could execute her design, she had to undergo a remonstrance from Mrs. Winston.

"And can the news I hear be true, dear mamma?" the latter asked.

"What news, Gertrude?"

"That Mildred is to be Mrs. Melcomb?"

"That is no news to you, Gertrude. You have known Mr. Melcomb's position here from the first."

"I knew he was idling about Mildred, as he has done about fifty other girls. But I did not know that she was to be sacrificed without her consent."

"Sacrificed, indeed!" exclaimed Mrs. Pendarrel. "Why, she has encouraged him!"

"No, mother," said Mrs. Winston; "never. She may lately have seemed to do so, owing to my advice. And she shall not suffer for taking it."

"Shall!" Esther repeated. "Upon my word, Gertrude, I could fancy you were practising the settlement of a daughter of your own."

"My dear mamma!" Mrs. Winston answered, in a tone which fully returned the sarcasm. "And you think Mr. Melcomb calculated to make Mildred happy?"

"Surely," replied the mother. "Is he not a highly agreeable and honourable man?"

"Agreeable, because he is a roué: honourable, because he does not cheat at cards. Is it not so, dear mamma?"

Mrs. Pendarrel smiled.

"You have been studying philosophy, my dear," she said; "taking a lesson from your own good husband. You know that scandal calls every handsome fellow a rake, and every generous one a gambler."

"I know nothing of the sort, but I know that Melcomb is both," said Mrs. Winston, very bitterly. "And I will do everything in my power to save my sister from the misery of such a union."

"You are a dutiful and grateful daughter, in good truth," cried Mrs. Pendarrel, with suppressed rage. "And, pray, what will you do?"

"I will at least offer Mildred a shelter in my house."

"'T will avail her nothing; the law is against you," the mother exclaimed furiously. "And for this I toiled and toiled, and placed my child in a position envied of a hundred rivals! For this I plotted, and manœuvred, and wasted hours and hours on that obdurate simpleton; and mined and countermined, and contended with dissension at home, and ill-dissembled malice abroad!"

"You might at least be respectful to your dupe, dear mamma, in my presence."

"Ungrateful! But why do I argue with you?"

Gertrude rose, and leant upon the back of her mother's chair.

"Because," she said, "you know that I am right. Mother, I have no reason to thank you for my marriage. You know it very well. It is true I have no such wretchedness to encounter as would befall Mildred in a match like this. The world thinks me a happy woman. I do not complain. I wear my chains as lightly and gracefully as I can. But they are chains, nevertheless. And you know it, mother. Yet I would fain think you meant me kindly, and it is therefore I remonstrate in poor Mildred's behalf. May we not discuss the affair as friends?"

"It is too late," said Mrs. Pendarrel.

"Too late!" Gertrude exclaimed.

"My word is absolutely pledged to Mr. Melcomb. It is impossible to recede."

"And Mildred only asked yesterday!" said Mrs. Winston, quitting her position, and walking away. "Sold, positively sold, for the contiguity of a few acres!"

But little more passed, before the mother and daughter parted with a very ceremonious salute.

Did Mrs. Pendarrel flinch under the remonstrances of her child? Did she waver a moment in her course? Reproached as the cause of Gertrude's unhappiness, did she hesitate to consummate the sacrifice of Mildred? If she had, she would not have been Esther Pendarrel. She had a quarrel with the world of five-and-thirty years' standing. Love! Folly! What had love been to her? Reason! She had married against it. Convenience! Ay, she wedded the heir presumptive of Trevethlan. So let her children. Had not Gertrude a house in Cavendish-square, and Winston Park, and a philosophical fool not ten years older than herself? Companionship—Ridiculous: there was plenty in the world. Home—Rococo: one lived abroad. With some soliloquy of this nature, did a withered heart excuse itself for spreading desolation like its own, conscious all the while that its pretences were false, saying, not thinking, the thing that was not.

Gertrude sought her sister on leaving Mrs. Pendarrel, and found her in a humour very different from what she had expected.

"So, Mildred, dear," she said, "we part. They take you to the enchanted castle, and where is the knight to wind the magic horn? Seriously, my poor sister, what will you do at Pendarrel?"

"Do, Gertrude!" exclaimed the younger sister, who might have been dreaming of the knight. "My despondency is gone. I am ready for the worst."

"And prepared...."

"Not to marry Mr. Melcomb, I assure you. You may lead a horse to the water, but who shall make him drink? All the vixen rises in my bosom, Gertrude. Mamma said something about my daring. I believe she has put me fairly upon my mettle, and will find I inherit it from her. So! Mildred!"

She flourished an imaginary whip. Her sister was perplexed, and a little troubled at her manner. She changed it suddenly.

"Oh, Gertrude!" she said, "do not think this levity comes from a light heart. I do know how hard a part I have to play. I do contemplate with sorrow this visit to Pendarrel,—so different from those in the old time, when we loved the country so much. With sorrow, but without fear."

"Ah, my sister!" said Mrs. Winston, "you are braver than I. See, you will be alone. Even Mr. Melcomb will not be there. You will be led on, and on, till you are completely entangled."

"No, no," answered Mildred. "And for him, I shall rejoice if he is away. He has had one chance of being generous, he will never have another. Who is so base as the man who would take a young girl's hand against her will?"

The sisters continued for some time in consultation, and parted with an oft-repeated embrace, and many promises of correspondence.

When Mrs. Pendarrel desired Mildred, on learning her attempted refusal of her suitor, to prepare for an immediate journey to Pendarrel, the one idea which arose in the young lady's mind was, that she should be near Trevethlan Castle. Many a train of thought developed itself from that suggestion, all ending in some vision of Randolph. And it was probably from such anticipations that she derived the seeming animation which perplexed her sister at this parting interview.

CHAPTER XVI.

Don John. Grow this to what adverse issue it can, I
will put it in practice. Be cunning in the working this,
and thy fee is a thousand ducats.

Borachio. Be you constant in the accusation, and my
cunning shall not shame me.

SHAKSPEARE.

Already the engagement of Squire Melcomb and Miss Mildred had been a
subject of discussion among the underlings of the establishment in May Fair,
and Michael Sinson, at least, had watched the signs of its progress with no
little interest. The announcement of Mrs. Pendarrel's immediate departure
for Cornwall, and the rumours which circulated that there the marriage
would be hurried forward as fast as possible, struck him with new
apprehension, as he feared that the great prize for which he was playing
might slip through his hands, merely from want of time to develop his game.
At all events, the move prevented him from indulging in the finesse which at
once advanced his object and gratified his vanity. Forward play was his only
chance, and he determined not to be defeated for want of boldness.

Sinson had fastened his clutches firmly upon the spendthrift, Everope. It is
so sadly easy to seduce, where the victim is prepared by need and unfortified
by principle. It was in vain that Everope, as often as the tempter forced a
new obligation upon him, vowed that he would only use it to support himself
until he could obtain some employment, and would then, by extreme
parsimony, save enough to repay his insidious creditor. The idea always came,
and was always chased away by the superior fascinations of the light pack
and rattling main. He could not be unlucky for ever. The first time fortune
favoured him, he would satisfy Sinson's claim, break off the acquaintance,
and abjure gaming for once and for all.

Fortune, however, frowned upon her votary with great perseverance. One
morning, after a turn of ill luck, when, in desponding apathy, wringing his
hands and calling upon Hercules, he was thinking of breaking with Sinson,
cost what it might, that individual crossed his path, and accosted him.

"What! is the goddess always blind, Everope? Nothing to be done at the
Rooms?"

"I shall go there no more," said the spendthrift sullenly. "I have done with
them, and play, and the world, and everything."

"Which means," Sinson observed maliciously, "that you have lost your money. Perhaps I can put you in the way of getting some. There's corn in Egypt."

"What can you do?" asked Everope. "Pick the lock of the granary, perchance? But I am desperate. Let me hear."

"Pooh!" said Michael. "I want a companion for a pretty long trip into the country. One not troubled with over-nice scruples; do you note me?"

"Then you may go somewhere else," cried Everope, who felt that he was selling his soul past redemption.

"And you will go into the Fleet," added the tempter, "to lie there till you die. Remember I have a considerable memorandum against you in my pocket-book; and I shall find a friend to serve me all the same. There's nothing that money won't buy; and there's plenty of it to be won here. I offer it to you in kindness, as a friend."

And he jingled some gold in his pocket to give emphasis to his words. Woe for Everope! He had made the step which costs: the rest were comparatively easy. "True," thought he, "if I hold back, another will be found. Already I am entangled with this scoundrel. And, after all, there may be nothing bad in the business. Pish!

'Returning is as tedious as go o'er.'"

That same night Sinson started with his victim for Cornwall. He found Everope quarters in a village at some little distance from Pendarrel, while he himself went to Wilderness Gate, where his aged grandmother received him with doting partiality. But he did not wish to attract more attention than he could help. He showed Everope about the neighbourhood of Trevethlan, pointed out the chief features of the locality, and in particular made him notice the approach to the castle.

There was no harm so far, and Everope rather marvelled that for this trivial survey he should have been brought such a distance. From Trevethlan Michael conducted his slave two or three miles along the coast to a cottage which stood somewhat retired.

"By the bye," he said, as they approached the modest dwelling, "I think you were at college, Everope. How long ago?"

"About twenty years," answered the spendthrift with a deep sigh.

"Was there any one there of the name of Ashton in your time?"

"I seem to remember the name," the spendthrift said, musing. "Ashton? yes, a rowing man, I think—yes, went into the church afterwards. I recollect now. But he was a good deal my senior. I knew but little of him."

"Did you ever hear what became of him?"

"Well, it was something strange," Everope continued. "Let me see. His family quarrelled with him. There was some story about his being murdered."

"Exactly so," said Sinson. "And we are now close to the scene. It was in this cottage that he lodged—just observe it—and some half mile from here along the cliff his body was found, nearly knocked to pieces on the beach."

The spendthrift's attention was excited by the tale, which also recalled those early days at college, when precocious dissipation and riot laid the seed of future ruin. Towards what abyss had he been travelling ever since? He seemed to turn round, and gaze backwards up a long slope, from the extremity of which his childhood looked down upon him still smiling and hopeful, but whereon at every pause in the descent he saw countenances more and more louring, and forms toiling upwards with averted faces. And now before him at a little distance, the incline was lost in darkness and clouds, and thitherward he was incessantly impelled, and there was nothing to stay his descent.

Sinson left him at his country quarters, merely saying, that they would return to London the following day, and that there Everope should learn the object of the journey. He himself repaired to the habitation of his grandmother.

The old woman was sitting in a rocking chair beside the fire, swinging herself backwards and forwards, and murmuring a hymn. She was little sensible to emotion now-a-days, but she rejoiced to behold her Michael again, and to perceive, what was evident even to her eyes, that he was a much finer person than when he went away. As he entered the lodge in the dusk of the evening, she ceased singing, and settled herself on her chair steadily, in order to look at him.

"Hither to me, my boy," said the old crone, stretching her shrivelled arm to reach a low stool and set it by her side; "come thee here to me. 'Tis dimly like, and my eyes get something old."

Michael, who had his reasons for humouring her, lighted a candle, and seated himself on the floor at her feet. She drew his head to her lap, and passed her hand lightly over his face, and then looked at him with eyes that were still bright and black, however she might complain of their decaying power.

"Ay," she said, with a smile, "he's just the same always, my Michael. And hast been to show thyself to Cecily, my boy?"

"No, grandame," he replied; "not just now. I have not the time."

"Not time to see thy mother, child? Cecily will fret when I tell her."

"That's just it, grandame," said Michael, "and so ye'd better not tell her at all. 'Tis a little errand for my mistress that I'm here for; and she don't wish it talked about."

"Well, well," mumbled Maud; "and Cecily was never like my Margaret. Dost mind Margaret, my boy?"

"Aunt Margaret was a fine lady, wasn't she, grandame?"

"Ay," muttered the old woman, recommencing to rock herself, "she was fit to be a queen. Didn't I read of her glory? But they took her away, and kept her all apart. 'T was long months I hadn't seen her, when I saw the dust thrown into her grave."

"And did you love Mr. Trevethlan, grandame?"

"Did I love the murderer of my girl?" Maud exclaimed, stopping her chair, and springing to her feet. "Should I love the murderer of his own wife? And didst not go with me when he was borne out in his turn? Was it tears we poured into his grave? Was it comfort we carried to his young son? Na, na. There's little love between Maud Basset and anything that bears the name of Trevethlan."

"Are you sure they were married?" Michael asked.

"Didn't I see it with my own eyes? Didn't I see how my angel blushed and trembled when he put on the ring, and he all so cold and stately like? Cursed be the gipsy babbler that bewitched his heart!"

"Folks say there was great doubt about it," observed Michael.

"They lie," said the old woman, again seating herself. "My Margaret *was* the lady of Trevethlan Castle, and cursed be they that turned her bliss to bane."

"Well, grandame," urged the young man, "would it not be a sweet revenge, to show that Henry Trevethlan deceived my poor aunt, and was himself deceived in turn, and so the children have no right to the name, and the lands pass away to strangers?"

"Is it her kinsman that speaks?" exclaimed Maud. "Is it the son of her sister would bring shame upon her memory? Is it a grandson of mine would defame my Margaret? Na, na. Thou'rt no Michael of mine. Out of my sight, viper, before I call the curse of Heaven upon thy head. Na, na. Let me go. Let me go."

And she quitted the room. But she came back again almost immediately.

"Ye did na mean it, Michael," she said. "Ye did na mean it. Good night to ye, my own boy. Good night."

"Good night, grandame," Michael answered, sulkily.

The next day he and Everope started on their return to London.

END OF VOL. I.

Milton Keynes UK
Ingram Content Group UK Ltd.
UKHW040311181024
449757UK00005B/487